W9-BTA-400

The
Secret Voice
of Gina Zhang

The Secret Voice of Gina Zhang

Dori Jones Yang

American Girl ™

Published by Pleasant Company Publications
Text Copyright © 2000 by Dori Jones Yang
Cover Illustration Copyright © 2000 by Emma Baker

Visit our Web site at **www.americangirl.com**

Printed in the United States of America.
First Edition
00 01 02 03 04 05 06 RRD 10 9 8 7 6 5 4 3 2 1

The characters and events portrayed in this book are fictitious.
Any similarity to real persons, living or dead, is coincidental
and not intended by the author.

AG Fiction™ and the American Girl logo are trademarks of Pleasant Company.

Editorial Development: Andrea Weiss
Art Direction and Design: Ingrid Slamer

Library of Congress Cataloging-in-Publication Data
Yang, Dori Jones.
The secret voice of Gina Zhang / Dori Jones Yang.—1st ed.
p. cm. "AG fiction."
Summary: When her extreme shyness makes her unable to speak at her
new American school, twelve-year-old Jinna, newly arrived from China,
retreats into her own fairy tale world.
ISBN 1-58485-203-8 (pbk) ISBN 1-58485-204-6 (hc)
[1. Chinese Americans—Fiction. 2. Schools—Fiction.
3. Mutism, Elective—Fiction.] I. Title.
PZ7.Y1933 Se 2000 [Fic]—dc21 00-028878

To my daughter,
Emily

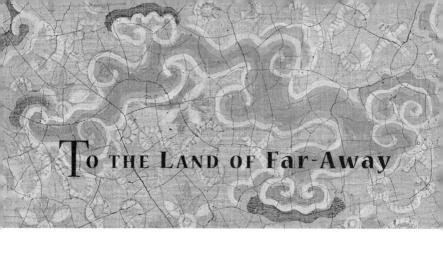

To the Land of Far-Away

THE SUN'S RAYS reflected off of the brilliant blue-black feathers on the Crow's back as he glided lower. The bird's giant wings spanned ten—no!—twenty times the width of a normal crow. He circled around the palace, spiraling down until he landed on the yellow-tiled roof.

The Princess, dressed in an elegant pink gown, played with her hoop in the palace courtyard. She laughed and ran. Suddenly, a huge shadow swept over her. Looking up, she cowered. The black bird swooped straight at her.

She raced across the courtyard for the palace door, but the Crow plunged down and grabbed her shoulders with his huge claws.

"No!" she shouted. "Put me down!"

He lifted her high in the air, laughing wickedly. She dangled, holding tightly onto his legs to keep from falling, and watched in horror as the palace grew smaller. They flew out over the city and the countryside, over orchards and fields and rivers and mountains, her skirt billowing around her legs and her long hair whipping across her face. At this height, she could barely breathe. The cold air pierced her lungs and made her cough.

"Where are you taking me?" she demanded.

The Crow suddenly plunged, so steeply the Princess thought she would slip out of his grip. He glided swiftly down till she could see a crowded marketplace in the distance. "Stop!" she shouted. "Take me back to my palace!"

But he kept flying lower, and soon he was swooping over the tops of people's heads. Some of the people screamed and ducked in his shadow.

Just above the most crowded spot,

the Crow dropped the Princess. Several arms reached up to catch her, and she landed in the midst of strangers, all shouting at once in a foreign language. Some people ran away in fear. Others held onto her, trying to get a closer look. An old lady felt the soft fabric of her dress. Another woman ran her fingers along the dragons and phoenixes embroidered on her skirt. An old man touched her jade hairpin. The Princess struggled and tried to run, but she couldn't get away.

"Let me go! I don't belong here!" the Princess cried.

CHAPTER one

THE DOOR TO Jinna's room opened and Mama's face appeared, smiling.

"Is everything OK in here?" asked Mama. "We need to leave in ten minutes. Have you brushed your teeth?"

"Yes," Jinna said, stuffing the Princess and the Crow under her pillow.

Mama came in and closed the door behind her. She sat on the floor next to Jinna and took her hand. "You're shivering," Mama said. "You should wear a thicker sweater."

"No, I'm OK." But Jinna didn't move to get up.

"Today will be a day you'll always remember, your

very first day at school in America," her mother said, squeezing her hand. "Auntie says it's a good school. Everyone says school is easier here than in China, so I'm sure you'll do very well."

Jinna nodded her head and bit her lip. Mama put an arm around her.

"You're lucky, moving to America as a child. Everyone says you will learn English quickly. I'll never learn to speak it right, but you'll be fluent in just a few years."

Mama's worry wrinkle appeared, and Jinna squeezed her hand back. She had heard this before from Mama and wondered why she kept repeating it. Were she and Father planning to rely on Jinna to learn perfect English?

"I'll be fine," Jinna whispered.

"By the end of the school year, your English will be better than Father's," Mama continued, her voice wavering slightly. "By June of next year, you'll be able to speak English better than Uncle and Auntie."

This seemed impossible. Uncle and Auntie had been in America more than six years. But Jinna nodded. Her mother always said encouraging things when she was anxious.

Jinna had never learned a new language before or even switched schools. What was hardest for Jinna was meeting new people.

Still, Jinna had already decided to put away the Old Jinna and be a new person in this new country. The New Jinna would fear nothing and no one. In this new country, Jinna wouldn't let anyone know how stupid and scared she felt all the time. She would make a good impression, and everyone would admire her.

Without realizing it, she took her hand from Mama and bit a fingernail.

"Don't worry," Mama pleaded. "Auntie says the children at this school are friendly, and they have a special teacher to help you learn English. You'll learn quickly."

"I'll learn quickly." Jinna parroted the words, sucking in strength from them. She turned and looked Mama in the eye. "You don't need to worry. I'll study hard and make you proud of me."

Mama's shoulders relaxed, and she smiled. "I know you will do well. Let's go."

They stood up. Jinna was almost as tall as Mama, but then, Mama was less than five feet tall.

Jinna ran a brush quickly through her chin-length black hair, smoothed the creases out of her new black pants, and grabbed her backpack, a blue one with freshly sharpened pencils and an unblemished pink eraser inside. She was glad her new sweatshirt had Tweety Bird on it. After all,

Tweety Bird was American, so Jinna would fit right in.

Just before leaving the room, Jinna tucked her fingers under the pillow and touched a soft piece of yarn from the Princess's gown. She straightened her shoulders and marched out the door.

It had rained overnight, and a light layer of leaves covered the grass in the yard. Mama zipped up Jinna's new jacket as if she were a first grader and not a twelve-year-old. She had made Jinna wear knit gloves, her first pair ever. Jinna's hands felt strange inside them.

A cold wind whipped Jinna's hair across her cheeks. Seattle in early November was much colder than her hometown in southern China.

"You fuss over her way too much," Auntie said, coming out of the house that Jinna and her parents shared with Auntie and Uncle. Then the three of them walked together the six blocks to Hilltop Elementary.

Mama held Jinna's hand tightly, as if Mama expected Jinna to slip on the wet leaves. Jinna tried to memorize the way, noticing a high hedge here, a red stop sign there, a square yellow house on the corner, a bush with bright red berries. The stop sign was the same shape as in China, but with an English word on it. They walked past rows of small, pretty houses with fenced-in yards and evergreen trees. In the spring, Auntie said, flowers would bloom everywhere. But right now the sky and streets were gray. Mama's gloveless hand trembled, and Jinna clutched it tighter.

A red-and-white-striped flag flew high above the school, visible from a block away. There were no other children on the streets. School had already started for the day. Why hadn't Auntie made sure they arrived on time, on her first day? It was bad enough starting in November, two months after the beginning of the school year. Did Jinna also have to start in the middle of the week, in the middle of the morning? But Jinna herself had insisted on waiting a few days, to get over jet lag, adjust to the new country, and build up confidence in the New Jinna. Today she was ready. If she waited even one more day, she knew that the old fears would set in and she would never make it.

Near the school a fat crow cawed and flew off a dumpster. Jinna froze, but Mama kept walking and gently tugged her along.

"Her name Zhang. Z-H-A-N-G." Auntie seemed so confident when she spoke English. Jinna wondered how long it would take to be able to talk to people the way Auntie spoke to the two women who sat at desks in the school's front office. One of the women was speaking English gibberish into a phone. *How can anyone understand it?* Jinna thought.

The other woman smiled at Auntie and asked her a question.

"Jin-na," Auntie answered, using the Chinese pronunciation of Jinna's first name.

The secretary strained her ears. "Jee-nuh? Jee-nuh?" Jinna's name sounded so different coming out of this lady's mouth.

Auntie nodded. After *Zhang,* the secretary wrote *Gina* at the top of a paper. "Gina Zhang," she said, mispronouncing Jinna's family name, too. She said "Zang" instead of "Jong."

The secretary smiled and said something to Auntie, speaking extra loudly and slowly, the way Americans do when talking to people who know little English. Her eyes, Jinna noticed, were light blue, a strange, transparent color.

"She says you have a pretty name," Auntie translated back to Jinna.

Jinna watched two girls in nearby chairs. One had a scraped knee, and the other was comforting her, waiting for the secretary to help them. One of the girls had wavy hair the color of straw. The other had very dark brown skin, darker than anyone Jinna had seen before, and kinky black hair in dozens of tiny braids. She noticed Jinna and smiled.

Jinna's heart began beating so hard she thought it would jump out of her sweatshirt. Everyone looked so different here in America. Did this girl think Jinna looked strange? But the New Jinna would not be afraid. She decided to smile back. By then, though, the girl had looked away.

Jinna didn't pay much attention to the questions Auntie was answering, the forms she was filling out, or the information the secretary was giving. Why should she? Everyone spoke in English. Jinna felt as though she were watching a foreign movie with no subtitles, observing people's faces and actions without understanding a word.

Suddenly Auntie was explaining to Mama, in Chinese, that they had assigned Jinna to a fifth-grade class, that the secretary would take her there, and that they should pick her up at three o'clock.

"But I'm in sixth grade!" Jinna protested.

"Sixth grade is at a different school, a middle school, too big and confusing," Auntie told her. "Since you don't speak English yet, we think it would be better for you to start fifth grade here."

Jinna shook her head. In an instant, she had been demoted to fifth grade. She hadn't been the best student in the class in China, but she didn't deserve to be put back.

Then Mama touched her shoulder lightly and squeezed her hand, saying, "It's for the best. Here's your lunch. Make sure you eat it all. I'll see you at three o'clock." Mama handed her the plastic container she had carefully packed with rice and dried fish and Chinese pickles that morning. Then Jinna watched in shock as Mama and Auntie walked out the door, turning to wave only once before disappearing. The New Jinna, the brave one, went with them, leaving the Old Jinna alone and scared in this strange environment where everyone spoke a language she didn't understand.

The blue-eyed secretary stood up and gestured for Jinna to follow her. The girl with the braids spoke to Jinna in an excited tone and waved good-bye.

Jinna felt embarrassed, unable to understand or answer. Her heart raced and she looked at the door. Could she run out quickly enough that no one could catch her?

Suddenly the secretary took her by the shoulders. She had fingernails that were long and painted dark purple. Jinna's mouth went dry, and her hands began to sweat inside her gloves, which she immediately took off and stuffed in her jacket pockets. The secretary pushed Jinna gently, and her feet began moving. The secretary spoke to her in a reassuring voice, the kind that adults use on kindergartners.

They walked down a hallway and turned. Jinna could see a huge open classroom with children sitting around tables, not at all like the neat rows of desks in her class in China.

They walked through what appeared to be a library—shelves of books, but no walls. It had three or four open classrooms surrounding it. *Why aren't there any walls?* Jinna thought with alarm. It didn't look like a school at all. She could hear children talking and laughing. Very few seemed to be reading silently or completing their work, as in China. How could anyone learn with so much noise?

The purple claws on her shoulder directed her to an open classroom on the far side of the library. A dark-haired woman was reading a book to a group of students sitting on the floor around her. Jinna thought she looked too young and pretty to be a teacher. She looked more like an actress or a singer. Other students sat writing at their desks, arranged in squares like tables.

The secretary said something to the young teacher with an apologetic tone in her voice. Jinna noticed a look of alarm on the teacher's face. The teacher sighed, flicking her elegant brown hair back over her shoulder.

She doesn't want me in her class, thought Jinna. *I wonder why. Maybe she doesn't like Chinese people.*

The secretary shrugged, and her purple claw let go of Jinna's shoulder, but Jinna felt like grabbing it back. The teacher gave Jinna a weak smile. Many pairs of eyes stared at her out of an assortment of strange-looking faces. There were only about thirty kids in the class—not sixty, as there had been in her class in China—and yet the room seemed crowded and the air too thick. Jinna couldn't breathe it in properly. Her throat felt like it was closing in on itself. She gulped in as much air as possible.

The teacher asked Jinna a question, but the secretary answered it for her and handed Jinna's folder to the teacher. Then the secretary left, and Jinna felt scared and alone in this sea of strange faces.

The teacher opened the folder, examined it briefly, and put it on her desk. She had little silver rings on every other finger.

She said something and gestured toward a space on the floor next to a big, tall girl with smooth brown skin and long hair that fell in soft black curls, very different from the tight braids of the girl Jinna had seen in the office. This girl's dark eyes had a friendly look to them, and she had a big, goofy gap between her front teeth. The girl smiled and eagerly patted the floor beside her. Didn't American schools have enough chairs? Jinna sat down, her skinny legs sticking straight out in front of her.

The teacher continued reading the book aloud. Jinna looked at her fellow students. Some of them were a lot bigger than fifth graders in China—taller and fatter. Some had very dark skin like the girl in the office, who, Jinna noticed, came into the classroom a few minutes later and sat at a desk. Other kids had faces that were pinkish, or pale, or shiny brown. Several had yellow hair, including one boy whose hair was almost white. One boy had orange hair. Another didn't seem to have any hair, as if it had been shaved off his head. Most of the kids wore blue jeans. Several kids wore glasses that made their eyes look oversized, and some had wires on their teeth decorated with bright colors. Some kids looked Chinese, or perhaps Korean or Vietnamese.

Jinna wasn't used to seeing people from outside her own province of Fujian, let alone people from other countries. She wondered if any of the kids spoke Mandarin or her dialect of Fujianese. When they asked or answered questions, of course, they all spoke in English.

And they sat too close to her. Jinna could feel the skin on the leg of the big girl next to her when the girl wriggled.

I am the New Jinna. I can get through this day, Jinna thought, taking in as deep a breath as she could and trying to convince herself. *These kids will learn to like me.* But she felt out of place. Sitting this close, she could tell that some of the kids smelled different. Often kids spoke out of turn, and the teacher reprimanded them. Yet they didn't seem to care about getting scolded. In China, if a teacher spoke to you like that, it meant you were in big trouble and would probably be punished.

The teacher said something, and everyone stood up. She pulled aside a girl with an Asian face and gestured for Jinna to come over to her. The teacher pointed to the girl and said, "This is Michelle." Jinna had no idea what the words meant, but her heart leaped. The girl looked Chinese. Perhaps she could speak to her and they would become friends. But when the girl opened her mouth, the words sounded unfamiliar. Jinna guessed the girl was speaking Cantonese, a Chinese dialect she didn't understand. She shook her head. The choking sensation returned to her throat.

The girl gestured for Jinna to follow, and the teacher nodded her head. So Jinna followed, with a group of ten or twelve kids, snaking through the hallways past other open classrooms, to a room at the far end of the building.

From looking at the faces in the classroom, Jinna guessed that this class was the special English class for kids from other countries. The teacher seemed delighted to meet Jinna. She had thick, curly white hair and the pinkest face Jinna had ever seen. She gave the other students a paper to work on and took Jinna aside. They sat down at a table.

"I am Ms. Linden," the white-haired teacher said, pointing to her chest.

Ai-em-iz-lin-din. It must mean "chest," Jinna thought. *These English words are so long. How am I going to remember that?*

"Your name is Gina?" the teacher asked. Her voice grew loud and slow.

Yur-nai-miz-jee-nuh. It didn't make any sense.

"Gi-na," said Ms. Linden, pointing at Jinna's chest.

Jinna looked down at her sweatshirt. It sounded like the teacher was saying her name, the way the secretary had pronounced it. But why was she pointing to Tweety Bird? Was this the way Americans pointed at themselves, instead of pointing to the nose as Chinese people did? A wave of humiliation washed over Jinna. She closed her eyes and wished that she could be magically transported back to her classroom in China.

"Hello," the teacher said. At last, a word Jinna recognized. Her eyes popped open.

"She wants you to repeat the English words she says." As if by miracle, one of the kids spoke to her in Mandarin. Jinna looked at all the faces in the class and tried to figure out who had spoken, but the teacher took her chin and turned her face back.

"You say, hello. Heh-lo," the teacher said, speaking loudly and slowly as if talking to a melon-head dummy. That's what Chinese children called an idiot. But her face was lit by a soft smile, and the white curls looked almost pretty. The wrinkles reminded Jinna of her grandmother.

Jinna opened her mouth. *Hello,* her mind said. But her throat was so tight no sound came out. The kids stared at her. It seemed to Jinna that they were judging her. They wanted to put her on a scale of 1 to 10, dumb to smart, stupid to fluent, bad to good.

"Heh-lo," the teacher said again. "I am Ms. Linden. You are Gina."

Hello! Jinna's mind was screaming now. *Hello! Hello! Hey-lo!* But the word wouldn't come out. It came up from her stomach and down from her brain, but the tightness in her throat kept it inside, churning and bouncing, trying to get out. *Hello! Hello!* What was wrong with her? Had she lost her voice?

Hello. Jinna mouthed the word.

The teacher smiled and nodded enthusiastically. Then she pointed to her ear and tilted her head closer to Jinna's face, saying something Jinna couldn't understand.

Another terrible wave washed over Jinna, and she felt like she was underwater, gasping and choking for air. *Hello* had stuck in her throat.

"Areyouallright?" The teacher's words made no sense, but Jinna could see the look of concern on her face. Then the pink face began wavering in and out of focus. What would this teacher think of her? Did she seem stupid? Were the other kids staring at her? They were surrounding her. She couldn't breathe. Her thoughts scattered far and wide. The teacher's face seemed to grow hideously big. Jinna stood up and backed away, knocking her chair over. She looked around desperately for a way out. Now the kids really *were* staring at her.

She began running blindly, back the way she had come, hoping to find the office and the front door at the end of the hallway. She slammed into a small kid and then into a teacher who tried to grab her. She struggled free and kept running, only to trip on her feet and fall in the middle of the library.

The librarian reached out to help her, but she pushed away the hands. A crowd of kids surrounded her, using strange words, reaching toward her. She got up and tried to ram through the bodies, but the librarian held her and guided her past the other kids.

There it was! The front door! She tried to make a

run for it, but she couldn't get out of the librarian's grip. The librarian led her to the front office, and then the secretary took her into a small room with a bed in it. The secretary sat Jinna down on the bed. Jinna tried to jump up and head for the door, but the secretary held her with those purple claws. *I've got to get out of here!* Jinna thought. *I can't breathe.*

The secretary pointed to the bed and said something. Jinna knew she was being told to stay there. But as soon as the secretary left to go get someone, Jinna glided to the door and opened it a crack. She watched the secretary go into another office. Then she sprinted out of the small room, across the main office, to the front door of the school, and outside.

Someone raced after her, shouting. It was a man, running with long strides. Before she reached the street, the man seized her shoulders and stopped her with a jerk. She nearly fell, panting and gasping.

He said something in a calm and gentle voice. He waited till she caught her breath, then clasped her hand firmly and walked her back into the building. He led her into an office, closed the door, sat her down, and sat next to her. She eyed the door and tried to calculate what it would take to get past him.

Again, he spoke in a kind voice. He was a tall man, with a thick chest, dark hair, and black wire-rim glasses. *Is he the principal?* Jinna wondered, her heart thumping wildly. In China, no one would dare run away from school. Anyone caught by the principal would be in big trouble. What had gotten into her?

Jinna hung her head. Father would be furious. What had happened to her plan to impress everyone with the New Jinna? She had done the dumbest thing of all, running from class, and shown all these kids—who were younger than she was!—how scared she was. Tears were building up inside her eyes, but she refused to let them roll.

The man didn't yell at Jinna, as a Chinese principal would have. Instead, he calmly asked questions. She shook her head, unable to understand or answer, and looked at the carpet. The colorful squares on it formed a pattern, and Jinna started to imagine a map of a faraway place, where every border was straight. No mountains, no winding rivers. Purple people lived in the purple squares; red people lived in the red squares. All the people were square-shaped but soft.

Finally the man gave Jinna a book with large pictures and a few words. She took it and pretended to look at it, relieved when his attention shifted away. He made a phone call and talked for a long time. Her heartbeat slowed. As long as she stayed in this office, with no one talking to her, she would be OK.

At one point the man stood up and offered his

hand. Did he want to take her somewhere? Probably back to class, Jinna thought. She shook her head and gripped the arms of her chair. He let her stay. She tucked her knees to her chest, protected from the outside world, and tried to make her mind go blank. *What a disaster. Mama will be so disappointed. She thought I would learn so quickly.*

From the window, Jinna heard a flutter and a light clunk. A crow had landed on the windowsill. He turned his head and aimed his beady black eye at Jinna. She froze. He let out a big caw and flew away. She wrapped her arms more tightly around her knees and closed her eyes. So this was what it felt like to go to an American school.

C HAPTER **two**

J INNA WAS STILL curled up in the chair in the office when Mama arrived.

With no English, Mama couldn't ask or answer any questions of the people at school. She just took Jinna's hand and led her home. Jinna's legs felt like wood as she walked, and she hung her head. The hurt felt like a hard fist squeezing her heart.

Fortunately, Mama had come by herself. Father would not have been so patient or understanding. He was learning to cook at Uncle's restaurant, a big adjustment from his office job back in Fujian. He and Uncle left the house at ten o'clock every morning and didn't get back till around midnight. Mama was helping at the restaurant, too, but she had rushed to Jinna's school as soon as Auntie got the call.

"What did you do?" Mama asked when they left the school. "Why were you in the school office? What kind of trouble did you get into, on your very first day?"

Jinna shook her head, her voice unable to escape.

When they got home, Mama went to the kitchen to prepare a meal of barbecued pork and rice. Jinna ran straight to her room and pulled the Princess out from under her pillow. She slid the Princess into her pocket, fingering the edges of the little skirt, while she waited for Mama to finish cooking.

The Princess didn't make stupid mistakes. She would have impressed all the teachers and kids at school, and everyone would have liked her. She wouldn't have been afraid.

Jinna tried to make sense of what had happened at school, but she couldn't. The whole day was like a dizzy spell or a nightmare. What was wrong with her throat?

Jinna had always been a shy person, even in China. For as long as she could remember, she had been uncomfortable talking to strangers, even to her own teachers. One incident, in third grade, especially stung in her memory. All the kids were silently working on an assignment in class one day, drawing pictures to illustrate the water cycle of rain and evaporation. As she worked, Jinna started to invent a story in her head about a little raindrop. She got so caught up in the story that she started talking aloud, in the characters' voices.

"But I'm just a little raindrop," she had said. "I've never jumped from a cloud before." She had spoken in a soft voice, not realizing that in the silence of the classroom, everyone could hear.

"But you must," she had answered in a deeper voice. "In a big rainstorm, we all must jump. Don't worry. You will come back to the sky again."

"I'm scared," her little raindrop voice continued.

Suddenly, she realized that the teacher was standing behind her, and all the kids in her third-grade class were staring at her.

"Little Raindrop," her teacher said. "Scared or not, you must jump." And all the kids burst into laughter. After that, everyone at the school heard the story, and the kids mocked her as "Little Raindrop." Even the older kids, fifth and sixth graders, singled her out and teased her. It didn't seem funny to her. She was sure they all thought she was silly and weird. She stayed away from other kids and stopped speaking in class, except when the teacher called on her. Then she answered in such a small voice no one could hear her.

But she had never actually lost her ability to speak—not until today.

Gradually, after eating, the tension in Jinna's throat eased and she told Mama what had happened on her first day at the American school. The smooth sounds of Chinese slipped out quietly at first, but easily. What a relief to get her voice back!

"Do you feel sick? Did anyone hurt you? Did a teacher yell at you?" Mama wanted to know. She seemed to imply that Jinna must not be telling the full story.

Jinna was embarrassed. No one had done anything bad to her. And she wasn't exactly sick. But how could she make Mama understand what it was like to be at school, expected to learn, and not able to understand anything or say anything?

"Auntie and I will take you back again tomorrow. This time, we'll go with you to your classroom, and Auntie will talk to your teacher."

"Please don't tell Father."

"Don't worry. I know how you feel. Just today I was in a store and I wanted to buy something, but I couldn't understand what the cashier said. The cashier repeated it slowly, as if I were stupid, but I still didn't understand. It's frustrating when you can't just say what you want, in Chinese."

"But it's worse than that for me. I couldn't say one word, even when I knew what to say."

"That's just nervousness on your first day. You've always been shy. It's natural. You'll adjust soon, and before you know it you'll be speaking English."

Jinna shook her head. Mama seemed so sure. But Mama had never been shy. She was always outgoing and talkative. In China, Mama always said shyness was attractive in a girl. Jinna remembered the tone of pride in Mama's voice when she told people how very shy her daughter was.

Mama finished washing the dishes, wiped her hands on a towel, and sat down opposite Jinna at the kitchen table. "I want you to do your old mother a favor," she said, her face smooth and round and her eyes sparkling. "Every day, I want you to teach me one new word in English. By June, I will know— how many? You tell me. Eight months times four weeks times five days in a week . . ."

"One hundred sixty words," said Jinna, smiling.

"I won't be fluent, but I'll know one hundred and sixty English words!" Mama said. "It's a start. What word did you learn today?"

"Hey-lo."

"No fair! I know that one already. Another!"

"Jee-nuh," she said, pronouncing her name the American way.

"What does that mean?" asked Mama.

"It's my name. Jinna. In English, they pronounce it Jee-nuh."

"Oh!" Delight washed over Mama's face. "Jinna. Jeen-nah." She couldn't get the sound quite right, but Jinna could.

"I am Jee-nuh," Jinna said, pointing to her chest instead of her nose.

"Ah um Jeen-nah," Mama mimicked, pointing to the neck of her own sweater.

"No! *You* are not Jee-nuh. I am!" Jinna corrected her in Chinese. Their laughter calmed Jinna's frayed nerves better than the pork and rice had. Maybe she could handle school after all.

Mama insisted that Jinna go to bed early that night. Alone in her bedroom, she thought again about the tightness in her throat and wondered if something was wrong with her. She hadn't simply refused to speak at school. She *couldn't* speak. It was frightening. But surely Mama was right. It was first-day jitters. Already her voice had come back. She'd be better tomorrow.

Jinna opened the drawer where she kept her yarn figures—kings and queens and demons and ogres and men and women. She had started making them years ago, with her best friend, Yinglan. Yinglan's mother worked in a sweater factory in Fujian, and she often brought home yarn that wasn't needed. She taught the two girls how to wrap the yarn into balls for heads and then make arms, legs, and bodies from yarn, using bits of fabric for clothes.

Jinna and Yinglan had spent hundreds of hours creating yarn dolls and playing with them, fashioning enough different characters to fill whole villages and making up stories and adventures about them. The girls called them "Yarn People" and even made furniture and houses for them. Jinna and Yinglan never told anyone outside their families about the Yarn People and their special world.

The Princess was Jinna's newest one, made by Yinglan as a going-away gift. She pulled the Princess out of her pocket now and smoothed her dress and hair. Then Jinna grabbed several handfuls of people and scattered them on the wood floor. That was the marketplace, and the Princess was lost in the crowd.

. . . "Where am I?" the Princess shouted above the horrible din.

"This is the Land of Far-Away, in the province called Over-the-Mountain," replied an old man near the front. "Where do you come from? We wonder about you, flying in on an evil crow like that."

"I am the Princess Jade-Blossom. I come from the City of Eternal Peace."

"Look at how royally she's dressed," said a young lady. "There are dragons and phoenixes embroidered on her skirt."

"Anyone can wear that these days," said an older woman. "I don't believe her."

"But only the royal family can wear five-toed dragons and yellow phoenixes," insisted the Princess.

"She flew here on a big black bird. That's a bad omen," said an old man. "She brings bad luck."

"Perhaps she's another monster! In disguise!" shouted a younger man. Several of the people backed away from her.

"Maybe she's come to help us fight the monsters," said a young woman wearing a simple blue dress.

"What if she really *is* a princess?" said a middle-aged man. "We should be nice to her."

"Of course I'm a princess. Can't you see that?" Jade-Blossom was confused and angry.

"Then tell us why you came," said the old man.

"The Crow brought me here. I didn't mean to come. Can't anyone help me get back to the City of Eternal Peace?" . . .

"Jinna!" Mama opened the door, and light from the hall flooded into the semi-darkness of her room. "You're playing! You should have had the light out by now. Put your toys away and get to bed at once."

CHAPTER **three**

J INNA WOKE UP early the next day and lay in bed for a while, thinking about the day before. What had scared her so much? These were kids and teachers, just like in China. Their school looked different and their faces looked different, but inside they must be ordinary kids just like her. They didn't know about the Little Raindrop story, and they never would. Nobody would think she was silly or strange. She would gradually learn English, and someday all that gibberish would make as much sense as Chinese.

Hah! As if that were possible. She took out the Princess and looked at her longingly. If only Jinna could just stay home all day and play with the Yarn People. Just for luck, she slid the Princess into the pocket of her pants. She wished she had jeans like the kids at school. And she wasn't sure if her Tweety Bird sweatshirt was really in style after all.

Over breakfast, Mama and Auntie gave Jinna a pep talk.

"School is like work, for children. It's the most important thing you do," Mama said, sounding suspiciously like Father. They must have talked about her last night. "You have to do your best and make our family look good in this new country." When Mama was stern her face looked like a round rock.

Jinna took another spoonful of rice porridge. She decided she would learn at least two people's names today—perhaps those of her teacher and the friendly girl with the tiny braids.

"Jinna! We're speaking to you!" Mama snapped.

Jinna looked up obediently.

"Today in class I want you to try to speak English. Even just one word, in a whisper. But really try, OK?" Now Mama's eyes were swimming with stern tears.

Jinna nodded.

"Answer me. I want to hear your voice."

"Yes, Mama. I will try."

Mama's face softened. "OK. It will be easier today, I'm sure."

"Don't worry, Mama." Jinna listened to the sound of her voice in Chinese. Had her voice box returned to normal? Or would it choke up again in school today?

"When I see you tonight," Mama said, "tell me what English words you said today. Remember to teach me at least one English word."

Jinna nodded.

"Ah ma Jee-nee," Mama said, pointing to her chest.

Jinna smiled at her pronunciation. Perhaps it was true. English would be even harder for Mama than for her.

Auntie and Mama walked with Jinna not only to school but into her classroom. The pretty young teacher stood up to greet them.

"Hello. I'm Ms. Armstrong," she said, pointing to her chest. Jinna knew now that the teacher must be saying her name. *Mizamustalang.* She tried to repeat it in her head so she wouldn't forget it.

Auntie spoke English to the teacher, apparently introducing Mama and then talking about Jinna.

What is she saying? Jinna wondered. *Will it help me or hurt me? How can Auntie explain my behavior yesterday? Is she telling her I'm not normal?*

Ms. Armstrong kept nodding her head, swishing her beautiful brown hair and sending gentle glances toward Jinna. She answered Auntie softly.

"Your teacher's very nice," Auntie reassured Jinna. "She promises she will help you."

"Be good today," Mama warned.

When Mama and Auntie left, Ms. Armstrong showed Jinna to a new desk that had appeared in the room. Then she brought over a very large boy with short stubby black hair. She kneeled down so she would be eye-level with Jinna, placing her hand with the silver rings on Jinna's new desk. Then she spoke to her in English.

"Uh, Teacher says welcome to our school," the boy translated in Mandarin. "She says she wants you to be comfortable here."

Jinna looked up at the boy's face, trying to remember exactly what he looked like so she could find him again if she needed to ask him questions. The teacher continued talking in a gentle tone.

"Teacher says other kids don't speak English yet either, so don't worry. Just do what the other kids do, and the ESL teacher will teach you English."

Jinna nodded to show she understood. *ESL.* Was that the special English class? The boy had called it ESL even in his Mandarin sentence. She wanted to ask the boy his name and wanted to ask if he could sit near her, but the words would not come out.

"You got any questions?" the boy asked.

Jinna shook her head no. The teacher smiled at her and patted her hand and said something in a reassuring tone of voice.

Why hadn't the words come, even in Chinese? Jinna was surprised and dismayed. This morning, at home, she had been able to speak. What was happening to her? She wished she could have thanked the teacher and the boy for their help. She wished she could easily open her mouth and say a word or two of English. Still, another part of her mind thought, maybe it was safer not to speak—not yet, anyway. As long as she said nothing, she would not make any stupid mistakes and no one would laugh at her. She wrapped her ankles around the bottom of her chair legs and hoped she wouldn't have to move all day.

But she did have to move. Every half hour, it seemed, the kids got up to sit on the floor near the teacher, to move to another desk to work on a project, to go to the library for a book, to leave the room for special classes, or to go to recess. Jinna was never sure whether to follow them or not, since different kids did different things. It was not like China at all, where everyone did the same thing at the same time.

At eleven o'clock, the teacher said a sentence with the word "ESL" in it, and nearly half the class stood up to leave. The Mandarin-speaking boy with the spiky hair came to Jinna's desk. "Now we go to English class. Follow me. My name's Henry." His tone wasn't very friendly, but at least Jinna could understand him. Jinna slipped her hand in her pocket and fingered the edge of the pink gown. The Princess whispered that she would go to English class with Jinna, eager to learn.

Today, I will speak in class, Jinna thought as she followed Henry. *Even if it's just one word, whispered, I will speak my first word of English.*

But the ESL teacher, Ms. Linden, had other plans. She made Jinna sit with two other kids from fifth grade who didn't speak English at all. One had an Asian face but didn't speak Chinese. Ms. Linden gave them each a set of alphabet letters and showed them how to put them in order, following a chart: A, B, C, . . . Jinna had learned this alphabet in China, where they used it to teach Mandarin pronunciation to kids who spoke a different dialect. After second grade, though, her teachers seldom used it, and she had never learned any English words with it.

Still, she had no trouble putting the letters in order. In fact, she finished before the other two kids and started helping them by pointing to the chart and finding letters for them.

Jinna hoped Ms. Linden would teach her a new word today. Jinna looked around the room at the English words pasted on the table, board, chairs, drawers, and clock and tried to make sense of them, but she couldn't. They just seemed like a stream of meaningless letters.

By the time Ms. Linden came back from teaching the more advanced kids at the other side of the room, all three of the beginners had their alphabet letters in order. Ms. Linden praised them, mixed up the letters, and made them do it again. Even though Jinna couldn't understand her words, she could tell by the way Ms. Linden moved her head and hands that she was thanking the other two kids for helping Jinna. It didn't seem fair, and the Princess jumped up to protest, but Jinna held her back.

At noon, Jinna followed the kids out of the ESL classroom and straight to the cafeteria. When she got there, she realized that she had left her lunch in the classroom, and now she didn't remember how to get back. Henry, the only person who could help her, ran off with some boys.

She stood near the door, feeling uncertain. The kids rushed to line up, passing a seated woman who took money from them or looked at a card. Jinna didn't have money or a card.

Suddenly she noticed the girl with the tiny braids

standing next to her, smiling. "Hi. I'm Sheliya," the girl said.

Shee-lee-yah. Jinna tried to repeat it to herself. She smiled shyly and nodded, assuming the girl was offering to help.

"Yougottacard?" Sheliya held up a plastic card and looked at Jinna with a question in her eyes.

Jinna shook her head no.

"Youneedacard. Comewithme." Sheliya led Jinna to the end of the line and talked to the cashier. The cashier wrote down Jinna's name on a slip of paper and gave it to Sheliya. The cashier seemed to be telling her to take it somewhere. Sheliya tried to explain the instructions to Jinna, who nodded as if she understood.

The cashier let Jinna go ahead into the cafeteria. Jinna followed Sheliya through the line, getting a tray and putting food on it. The food was strange— some sort of large, hard yellow cracker, folded in half, with meat and raw vegetables in it. The milk came in small brown cartons.

Sheliya led her to a table with several girls from the fifth grade. Jinna sat near the end. The other girls chatted happily while Jinna stared at her food, trying to figure out what it was. She opened her milk carton and smelled chocolate.

Jinna noticed that the other girls ate with their

hands, not with a fork, so she picked up the large cracker and took a bite. The taste wasn't too bad. She chewed it for a while, then a while longer before she realized she could not swallow. She kept chewing, till the cracker was soft mush in her mouth, but her throat would not open.

Sheliya noticed. "You don't like tacos, huh?"

Jinna smiled and nodded, hoping this was the right response to whatever Sheliya had said.

Some of the other girls tried speaking to her in different languages—Vietnamese, Korean, Cantonese. Jinna could tell that they weren't speaking English, but she didn't understand a word. She kept chewing the same bite.

"Hey! Henry!" Sheliya grabbed at Henry as he walked behind her with his empty tray, heading for the door. "You speak her language, don't you? Ask her what her name is."

"Her name is Gina. Teacher tell us that," he said, looking uncomfortable in the girls' presence. He wriggled away without speaking a word to Jinna.

"OK. Here goes." Sheliya smiled at Jinna. "I am Sheliya." She spoke slowly, pointing to her chest. "Coolest girl in the fifth grade." She flashed a grin at her friends and then at Jinna.

Jinna smiled and nodded. This girl wanted to be her friend.

Sheliya pointed to Jinna's chest and said, "Gina." Then she pointed to herself and said, "Sheliya."

Jinna nodded. *Shee-lee-ya,* she thought. It wasn't a hard name to say. It sounded like it could be Chinese. But the word got stuck in her throat like a chicken bone.

The girl with the wavy blond hair rolled her eyes and gave a big, exaggerated sigh. When she stood up to leave, all the other girls did, too.

Sheliya looked at Jinna's blank face and then at the other girls. "Seeyalater," she said to Jinna, with a shrug of her shoulders. She followed the other girls as they dumped their garbage, stacked their trays, and ran out the door, jabbering in English the whole time.

See-ya-lay-ta. I bet that means good-bye. Jinna stayed put, chewing the same bite. Part of her was sorry to see them leave, but the rest of her was glad to be out of the spotlight. She spit the bite out on her plate and took a sip of chocolate milk. To her relief, the milk went down. Her throat wasn't totally broken. But what was wrong with it?

She thought about the fishing birds in China, cormorants. Fishermen put metal bands around the cormorants' necks so when the birds caught a fish, they couldn't swallow it. She fingered her neck, half expecting to feel a metal band.

At the far end of Jinna's table, another girl sat alone. It was the tall girl she had sat next to on the floor of Ms. Armstrong's classroom. The girl looked sad and lonely. She was busy pushing food around her plate, her mouth moving as she talked to herself nonstop. Jinna marveled at her hair, which was long and thick and curly, not short and straight like Jinna's.

The girl lifted up her fork mid-sentence and noticed Jinna looking at her from across the long table. When she smiled, Jinna noticed again the huge gap between her two front teeth.

The girl leaned on the table and stood up, then lumbered toward Jinna, dragging her tray with her. She threw a long leg over the bench and sat down next to Jinna.

"You're Gina, right? I'm Priscilla," she said.

Pa-see-la, thought Jinna, smiling at the girl and nodding. *Can I remember this one?*

But Priscilla didn't wait for a response. "I sat next to you yesterday when Ms. Armstrong was reading *Under the Blood Red Sun.* I like that book, don't you? I can't imagine what it was like to live during a big war like that."

Jinna didn't understand a word Priscilla had said but liked the way she said it. Priscilla just seemed to assume Jinna got it. She barely paused for breath.

"But I don't like baseball, do you? I don't like any sports. I hate it when someone throws a ball at me. Why do people always have to throw balls at you in sports? Is that supposed to be fun?"

Priscilla looked at Jinna as if she expected a response, so Jinna smiled and nodded.

"Maybe you like sports, but I don't. I don't see why everybody has to play sports. It's like they expect you to find it fun. Whiz, whiz"—Priscilla's hand zipped back and forth like a ball at a soccer match—"the ball shoots around and you're supposed to go after it. Me, I don't want to go after it! I'd rather run away from it! Really, think about it. A ball comes straight at you. Wouldn't you want to run away from it before it hits you?"

Jinna nodded vigorously, enjoying the attention, wanting to listen more, and glad she wasn't expected to answer. For the first time, English didn't sound so harsh and foreign. And Priscilla seemed happy to have found such an eager listener.

"Even those balls on ropes, tetherballs. You think they're under control, attached to the pole like that. You hit it and guess what!" Priscilla's eyebrows went up as she paused for effect. "It comes around and hits you in the back!" She circled her hand slowly, then banged herself on the back of the head and made her eyes go googly.

Jinna laughed. Priscilla laughed, too, a high-pitched tee-hee-hee that made Jinna laugh harder.

"But kickball is the worst." She was nearly whispering now, as if Jinna were in on a secret. "I never play it, except in P.E., when we have to. You know what those boys do?"

Jinna looked at her with wide, expectant eyes.

"They say,"—here Priscilla switched into a high-pitched mocking voice—"'This one's for you,' and they kick it as hard as they can, straight at me. One time a ball hit me smack in the face, like this." She opened her fingers wide and slapped herself hard on the nose. *It must hurt,* Jinna thought, with alarm. *Why is she doing this?* But she laughed anyway, since Priscilla let out a loud tee-hee-hee.

"So now do you know what I do?" Priscilla's voice dropped and she slid closer to Jinna, so no one would overhear. She needn't have bothered. All the other kids had left the cafeteria for the playground. Only the workers were left, clearing the trays and wiping the tables. "I run the other way!"

She leaned back, watching for Jinna's reaction. Jinna opened her eyes as wide as she could, as if she were shocked.

"One time, though, that boy Jeremy—you know Jeremy, right?—he kicked the ball at me. I turned to run and guess what!"

Gay-suh watt! thought Jinna. *Wonder what that means.*

Priscilla whispered loudly into Jinna's ear. "The ball hit me on the butt!" She waited for a reaction, then giggled. "I was so mad at Jeremy. I ran after him and started hitting him, but he just laughed. The other boys laughed, too. 'She loves you, Jeremy. She loves you!' they all shouted. Now I just ignore them all. They're such jerks. I hate kickball." Priscilla leaned back, pleased with herself.

Jinna nodded and smiled, wishing Priscilla would keep talking. She loved watching Priscilla act out her story, changing voices and using her arms.

"But you know who I really hate?" Again, Priscilla was whispering in her ear. "Kylie! You know which one she is? The one who was sitting here before, with the blond hair like this?" Priscilla's hands made exaggerated waves on her head. "She's the teacher's pet. You can tell. Ms. Armstrong always asks her to water the plants."

Jinna gave Priscilla a blank look and took another sip of chocolate milk. It went down her throat, smooth and rich as sweet warm soy milk.

"You don't know which one she is, do you? Well, I'll point her out to you. Stay away from her. She's trouble. Everybody thinks she's so pretty and nice, but she's not. One time I had this lead pencil, see?

You know, the kind you put the lead in? A new one, very cool, pink and teal. I had it about a week, and suddenly it disappeared. Guess what!"

Gay-suh watt! thought Jinna, with a smile. There was that word again. She had to find out what it meant.

"A week later I saw Kylie using it!" Priscilla waited for Jinna's reaction. Jinna could tell from her face that she should look shocked, so she did. Priscilla was pleased. "The little thief. Thinks she's so great."

A bell rang, so loudly Jinna jumped. Kids started streaming in from the playground, and Priscilla stood up, so Jinna did too.

"We gotta go. Nice talkin' to ya!" Priscilla took off without waiting for Jinna, as if she wasn't used to walking with other kids. But Jinna didn't feel abandoned. Perhaps this girl would be her friend.

Jinna thought about her throat. Was it getting better now? The cafeteria was so noisy with rushing kids that no one would hear her if she spoke.

Gay-suh watt, she tried to say. Her lips moved, but the sound didn't come out. *Gay-suh watt.* She put her hand on her voice box, but it didn't vibrate. The English words slid back down into her empty belly and fell flat. She squeezed her throat as if to punish it. *Stupid throat!* she thought. *You'd better start working, or else!*

CHAPTER **four**

THAT AFTERNOON, Jinna watched the clock hands move. She had promised Mama to say at least one word by the time Auntie arrived at three o'clock. But Ms. Armstrong ignored Jinna most of the afternoon.

Finally, when the other kids had started a writing assignment, the teacher came to her desk and handed her some flash cards. Each card had a colored picture on it—a butterfly, a boat, a girl, a cat, a dog, a monkey, and a pig. Under the picture, there was an English word. Jinna tried to remember the sounds of the letters. Priscilla came over once and looked at the cards. Jinna smiled, remembering how friendly she had been at lunchtime.

"Cool! I wish I could play with these instead of writing in my journal about my goals for fifth grade," Priscilla said.

Jinna pointed to the word under the monkey picture and raised her eyebrows in a question.

"Monkey," said Priscilla.

Mung-kee, thought Jinna. She moved her lips. *Mung-kee.* The sound stayed deep in her throat.

She pointed to the word under the pig picture and looked at Priscilla again.

"Pig," said Priscilla. "P-I-G, pig."

Pig, thought Jinna. *Pee-gu.* She laughed. It sounded almost like the Mandarin word for *butt.*

"What? What's so funny?" Priscilla shot her a sharp look.

Jinna hung her head to hide her smile.

Priscilla turned and walked away as if insulted.

What did I do? thought Jinna. After that, Priscilla didn't pay attention to her. Nor did anyone else. Jinna practiced *pig* and *monkey* and *Sheliya* and *guess what* in her head, planning to teach them to Mama that night. She wasn't sure she remembered the right way to pronounce Priscilla's name. But she would tell Mama the girl's name was *Guess What.* Mama wouldn't know the difference.

* * *

That weekend, Jinna spent most of her time in her uncle's restaurant, which was in Seattle's Chinatown neighborhood. Mama wouldn't let her walk around on the streets alone, but on Saturday Mama took Jinna with her when she went out to buy vegetables. Jinna loved looking in the shop windows and reading the signs—in Chinese!—and helping Mama pick out familiar-looking vegetables and fruits. One store was filled with Chinese books, and Jinna convinced Mama to buy a new book from the Monkey King series. The illustrations were wonderful, bright, and detailed.

Back at the restaurant, while she sat waiting on a chair, Jinna read the new book and examined the pictures. Like many Chinese children, she loved the characters of Monkey King and Pigsy the best. Pigsy was so fat and funny, so friendly and loyal, and Monkey King had fantastic magical powers.

As Jinna looked at the pictures, she got an idea. What if she could make Yarn People that looked like Monkey King and Pigsy and make them part of her Princess story? That would make it so much livelier. Yes! That was a great idea!

She peered closely at the pictures of Monkey King and Pigsy, noticing the way they looked and talked. How would they fit into her story? Her story would not be like the one in the book, a long journey with many battles. And most of the Monkey King stories didn't have any girls or women in them at all. Jinna's story would be different—a story with the Princess at the heart of it. Monkey King and Pigsy would just have to get used to that.

Making a yarn version of Pigsy would not be hard. In the book, he was gray, and she had plenty of gray yarn. But how could she ever make a decent Monkey King? The hardest part would be the face, which in the book was multicolored.

And when would she have a chance to make both of them? Weekends were the busiest days at the restaurant, and Mama didn't want to leave her at home for so many hours. Jinna longed for some time alone in her room.

Finally on Sunday evening, Jinna was able to work on Pigsy and Monkey King. She finished Pigsy in about half an hour. Then she started on Monkey King. She used mainly brown yarn and did the face ten times before she was satisfied. She'd never spent so much time making a Yarn Person, and as she worked she realized how terribly she had missed it.

On Monday, in ESL class, Ms. Linden took Jinna aside and spent ten full minutes with her. She made Henry translate.

"Each of the letters has a name and a sound," she said. "First I'll say the name, then I'll say the sound. You repeat. Tell her that, Henry."

"Teacher's gonna say something. You better say the same thing, or you'll get in trouble," Henry translated in Mandarin.

"A. Aaaa," Ms. Linden said, naming the letter and then making the short "a" sound in "at." That sound sounded strange to Jinna—not at all like the "ah" sound she had learned for the letter A.

Jinna opened her mouth wide to say "Ay" and "aaaa." But no sound came out.

Ms. Linden looked at her patiently. "A. Aaa. You'll have to say it louder."

Jinna shaped her mouth like an A and forced air out of her throat. It sounded like a cough. The imaginary metal band clenched tighter around her neck. She slipped her hand into her pocket and felt the Monkey King's legs and arms, tied with a yarn knot at each end. *Give me your magic, Monkey King,* she thought. *Please open up my throat. I've known the alphabet for years. I've got to let her know this.*

"I know you can do it, Gina. Keep trying. Here." Ms. Linden switched to a different card. "B. Buh-buh-buh."

These sounds were easier, but they couldn't get past the metal band either. Jinna pursed her lips and then opened them, as the teacher had. A breathy "heee" sound came out.

"Nobody can hear you," said Henry in Mandarin. "You better try harder or everybody will think you're a melon-head dummy."

Was everyone watching her? Did they all think she was dumb? They weren't laughing at her now, but they would once Henry told them she couldn't make a single sound.

"Try again," said Ms. Linden. "Bee. Buh."

Jinna pursed her lips for the B sound, but this time even her lips wouldn't open. She shook her head and pleaded with her eyes. *No more. No more. Please don't make me do this.* She wished she could be strong and confident, like the Princess.

Ms. Linden tried a few more letters, but Jinna didn't even open her mouth. Finally Ms. Linden leaned back with a gleam in her eyes. "Hmm. I had a student like you once before. Henry, ask her if she has trouble speaking at home."

Henry translated, and Jinna shook her head.

"Has she been able to speak at all since she got to school?"

Jinna shook her head again. Perhaps this teacher would understand. Perhaps this teacher would see behind the silence and know there was a normal person, not someone dumb and strange. All Jinna needed was some time and space, a chance to get used to this faraway world.

"Tell her this story, Henry. Five years ago one of my students had this same problem. It was a girl, too, from Somalia, I think. I don't know what kind of horrors she had seen in her home country. On the first day, she couldn't make a single sound."

Henry translated, and Jinna began to feel hope trickle through her veins.

"Day after day I worked with her, for weeks, months, more than a year."

Jinna's heart began to feel heavy.

"I spent more time with her than anyone. Finally, after two years of total silence, she spoke in class! I was so moved, I cried. She cried. Her classmates cheered. We were all so happy." The pink face grew soft and weepy.

Listening to Henry's translation, rough as it was, Jinna felt alarmed. Would it take two years before her throat opened up?

"You can do this too, Gina. I will teach you to speak English." Ms. Linden looked triumphant. "See this classroom? This will be the place where you say your first words in English. Even if it takes a long time, we can do it!"

The words, intended to cheer her up, depressed Jinna. A long time? Jinna thought this problem would disappear any day now. What would Mama and Father say if she didn't learn to speak English for two whole years? Perhaps Henry had translated wrong. She wanted to ask him but couldn't.

"Then again," continued Ms. Linden, looking around the classroom, "I had fewer students in those years. Only a handful, really. It will be much harder with twelve kids in the class."

"She says she has too many students now," Henry translated. "Probably she can't teach you very well after all. You're too late."

Jinna looked at Ms. Linden and at Henry and back again. Ms. Linden looked sad. Monkey King was ready to jump out with his long stick and do battle with the teacher, but Jinna wouldn't let him.

"We'll do our best," Ms. Linden said, patting Jinna on the hand. She stood up and walked across the room, too far to hear what Henry said next.

"No hope for you," Henry translated, laughing loudly enough to attract the attention of the kids sitting nearby. "This one can't even make a single sound," he whispered to them in English. "Dumb, right? Or maybe just"—he leered at her—"shy."

Sha-yee. Jinna could tell by the way Henry said this English word that he meant to insult her. It sounded a little like the Chinese word *sha,* meaning "stupid." Who was he to call her stupid? What if he was right?

What would the Princess have done at a moment like this? Jinna thought it over but couldn't come up with an answer. One thing she knew for sure: Princess Jade-Blossom would never let people make fun of her.

The other students laughed and started jabbering in broken English and bits of their own languages. Jinna's spirit sank down, through her feet, through the floor, deep into the earth. Only the outside of her body was left, and her throat was choking her. She wished she could faint or go invisible, but the next best thing was to remain still and silent. If she had the powers of the Monkey King, she could transform herself into a chair or a desk or a light fixture. Or better yet, a mosquito, and then she'd buzz out the door and no one would stop her.

CHAPTER **five**

. . . SUDDENLY a big-eared gray pig stood in front of the Princess.

"Come with me," he said. His appearance was strange, but his manner was so gentle and open that the Princess was inclined to trust him. Anything to get away from this unfriendly crowd.

"Where do you want to take me?" she asked, still unsure and shaken by the doubts of the crowd.

"I know someone who can help you." Pigsy pointed to a pagoda on top of the hill. "But you must be careful," he added. "If you are not really a princess, he will know right away."

"I am not afraid. I am the Princess Jade-Blossom."

Eager to get away from the crowd, she started to walk up the hill with the strange creature. "Who is he?"

"He is the Monkey King. He has magic powers."

"I have magic powers, too," said the Princess.

"Oh." The pig stopped. "Then you won't be needing the help of the Monkey King. You can get back to the palace on your own."

"That's true," said the Princess. Why hadn't she thought of that? In all the excitement, she had forgotten her own powers. She spread out her arms like wings and closed her eyes. *I wish to fly back to the palace,* she thought. But when she opened her eyes, she had not moved. Pigsy looked at her with pity, and she could hear laughter and jeers from the people in the square.

"If you're not a true princess, Monkey King will not help you," Pigsy said. "Once he sees that you have no magical powers, he will make you prove yourself a princess."

"But I am a true princess! Someone has taken away my magic. Please take me to him. I'm sure he will understand."

Pigsy hesitated, but when he saw the frightened look in her eyes, he held out his hand to the Princess. She took it and followed him up a steep hill. At the top, Monkey King waited in a beautifully painted wooden pagoda.

"Oh, great Monkey King, I am the Princess Jade-Blossom," the Princess said, trying to control her shaking hands.

"Call me Immortal Master Sun Wukong." With his multicolored face, the Monkey King looked like a clown, but he tried to command respect.

"Immortal Master Sun Wukong. I find myself far from my father's palace. Would it please you to help me find a way to get back?"

"Address me as Immortal Master Sun Wukong, King of the Water Curtain Cave, from the Mountain of Flowers and Fruit."

The Princess tried not to smile. She knew she must show Monkey King respect, no matter what he wanted to be called. "Immortal Master Sun Wukong, King of the Water Curtain Cave, from the Mountain of Flowers and Fruit, my father reigns as king in the City of Eternal Peace. I need to return to my home, the palace, where I belong."

"I do not believe that you are the Princess Jade-Blossom." Monkey King's red-and-yellow-rimmed eyes sparkled with mischief.

"Surely, oh Wise One, you who sees all! Surely you can see my true nature!" protested the Princess.

"The people of this town doubt you are the Princess. You will have to prove yourself to them."

The Princess held her head high. "A princess does not have to prove anything."

"A true princess would not mind being asked. It would be easy for her." Monkey King wrapped himself around his long, pointed stick and turned into a snake.

She drew back from the snake, wondering if it could harm her.

"Why don't you use your magic?" it hissed.

"I think someone has taken away my powers."

The snake hissed again and then turned into a white-bearded old priest. He stroked his beard and spoke slowly. "Then you must take three tests. Do you find tests hard?"

"In my palace, I took tests often and always did very well."

"This is not the palace," said the priest. "The rules are different here." The priest puffed on his pipe.

The Princess felt nervous. "I won't have to fight monsters, will I?" She had no interest in fighting.

"I alone decide what kind of tests you must take!" The old priest took another puff from his pipe and vanished into the smoke.

"Pigsy, this is unfair! He knows I am a princess, doesn't he? Why do I have to prove myself?"

Pigsy stood there with his only weapon, a rake. "I will help you," he said.

The Princess laughed and kissed his fat cheek. "Thank you, Pigsy. But whatever these tests are, I am sure I can handle them." . . .

Jinna's door opened. She looked up. Her father's sturdy frame filled the doorway.

"Come into the kitchen. I want to talk to you." A hard edge to his voice made her hesitate. But she had no choice.

Mama and Auntie were sitting at the kitchen table, looking sad.

"We just got a call from your teacher. I hear you are making trouble at school."

Jinna kept silent.

"I hear you refuse to speak." Father's voice grew louder. "Is this true?"

"It's not that she refuses to speak. She can't," Mama said softly.

"I want to hear Jinna explain! Are you disobeying your teachers?"

"No." Jinna's voice was so soft Father could barely hear it.

"Speak up!" he said. "There is no reason for you to stop speaking. I don't want the Zhang family to look bad. If you don't succeed in school, you have no future. Starting tomorrow, you will speak in school like a normal child."

Jinna said nothing.

Father shook his head and softened his voice. "It's difficult. I know English is very hard to learn. But you are young, and you will learn it quickly. We have to succeed in this new country. Tell me you will speak in school."

"I will speak in school." There was no point in contradicting him. Mama smiled her support.

"Reassure me by saying it again."

"I will speak in school."

"A third time, louder."

"I will speak in school." Her voice sounded tinny and fake.

"I don't want these Americans to see my child acting abnormal. Now go get ready for bed and turn the light off. No more playing."

Jinna sighed as she returned to her room. Father was like that. Whenever there was a problem, he issued an order to fix it. He meant well, Mama kept telling her, but to Jinna it seemed he was always barking commands. She wondered if all fathers were like that.

But even Father could not control Jinna's throat. It remained constricted the next day, the next week, the next month. After the first few days, Jinna had stopped trying to speak. Why bother? Every time she did, it ended in frustration and embarrassment.

In class, she listened carefully and learned as much as she could, but who can handle fifth-grade work in a language you barely know? Some days, she felt as if she must have left her brains back in China. Only math was easy because the numbers were familiar. But many of the math questions were word problems, with long sentences in English.

In ESL class, Ms. Linden relentlessly pushed Jinna to speak, as if she was hoping to be the first to hear Jinna's voice. But her voice simply wouldn't cooperate.

Jinna's father bought her a dictionary, but she found it very hard to use. After school and during winter break, her parents made her do Chinese homework so she wouldn't forget how to read and write in Chinese. But they couldn't help her with her American schoolwork, and they acted as if they expected she would just figure it out on her own.

Most of the kids, including Sheliya and Kylie, gave up trying to be friendly and just ignored her. How can you make friends with someone who doesn't talk to you?

Only Priscilla didn't mind. She continued to eat lunch with Jinna every day, talking on and on about nothing special. She told Jinna about her cat, Miss La Tabbette, nicknamed Tabby, and her hamster,

Fuzzface. She recited a long list of candy that she liked, starting with Milky Ways, and vegetables that she hated, starting with broccoli, and described which fast-food restaurants she preferred and why. She related long, involved stories she had seen on TV the night before, mixing people up and making up the parts that she forgot.

Jinna had no idea what Priscilla was talking about but listened carefully, picking up a key word here and there. *Meelky Waze. Baga Keeng. Whatevah.* She taught them to Mama but sometimes had to make up the meanings. Milky Ways she had tasted, but *Baga Keeng,* she told Mama, was a palace, and *Whatevah* meant "I can't remember any more."

Watching Priscilla's hand gestures and vivid facial expressions, Jinna understood a little more English every day. She learned more, in fact, from Priscilla than she did from Ms. Linden. She still didn't know the meaning of *Guess what!* but looked forward to hearing Priscilla say it. It was always followed by something that made Priscilla laugh her high-pitched laugh.

The other kids, Jinna noticed, avoided Priscilla. No one else wanted to sit with her at lunch or play on the bars with her at recess. Often when Priscilla started to talk to someone, that person would turn away in the middle of whatever Priscilla was saying.

When the fifth graders lined up, other kids would push and jostle each other to avoid standing next to Priscilla, who was taller and heavier than most of them. Sometimes she would lunge at them to frighten them, and they would run away as if scared of her germs. Then they would turn around, point, and laugh at her.

Jinna heard other kids say Priscilla's name in a taunting tone of voice. At home, she practiced the name and taught it to Mama.

"Pasilla," she said.

"Pa-see-la," Mama repeated.

One day in January, at recess, Jinna and Priscilla were sitting at the edge of the playground, near the door. Priscilla was scratching lines on the cement with a thick stick, talking nonstop as usual.

"Wanna hear a secret? Promise not to tell," she started. She pulled out a hair ornament, a butterfly clip with floppy wings. "Recognize it? It belongs to Sheliya. I found it in the bathroom. I'm going to show it to her, but I won't give it back unless she sits with me at lunch. Do you think that's a good idea?"

Jinna listened to the English words, arranging them in her head. This clip belonged to Sheliya, and Priscilla wanted to sit with her at lunch.

"I like Sheliya. I think she's a nice person inside," Priscilla continued. "But don't worry. I like you best.

You're my best friend." She gazed at Jinna solemnly.

I like you best. You're my best friend. In her mind, Jinna repeated the words in Chinese, then translated them back into English. Priscilla, pretty Priscilla with the curly black hair and lively, funny way of speaking, liked other girls, but she liked Jinna the best. She considered Jinna her best friend.

A smile of wonder spread across Jinna's face, and tingles ran up and down her arms and legs. Priscilla was her best friend. But even more important, Priscilla spoke to her in English, and she understood. Almost every word. *I understand English,* she said to herself, in English. *Pasilla is my best friend.*

She reached out to squeeze Priscilla's hand, to show that she understood. Priscilla looked her in the eye and squeezed back, grinning that goofy grin. *She knows I understand her English words,* thought Jinna.

Just at that moment, Kylie came rushing out the door and tripped on Priscilla's stick. She fell awkwardly and scraped her knee, which bled a little.

"Owwww!" she shrieked. "Priscilla, look what you did!" Kylie sat back and cradled her knee, dabbing at the blood. "It's bleeding!"

"Real smooth, Kylie," said Priscilla. "It's not my fault you didn't look where you were going. Tell my stick you're sorry." Priscilla poked Kylie gently with her stick.

"Ow! Get away from me!" said Kylie. Then, noticing Jinna at Priscilla's side, she added, "You know Gina's not really your friend, don't you? She only sits with you because she can't speak English yet. Once she learns how, she won't be your friend anymore, just like Michelle. You know that, don't you, Priscilla? Don't you?"

Jinna couldn't believe the mean tone in Kylie's voice. Almost instantly Priscilla's face turned a ferocious shade of red. She jabbed again with the stick, this time with force. Kylie tried to grab it and broke the end off. Angrily, Priscilla took the stick and was about to poke Kylie again just as Ms. Armstrong came out the door.

Kylie howled in pain.

"Kylie, what's wrong?" Ms. Armstrong asked. "Priscilla, what on earth are you doing with that stick?" Priscilla jumped up and ran away across the playground.

"She tripped me, Ms. Armstrong," Kylie whined. "Then she poked me with that stick. Look, my knee is bleeding!"

"Let me see." Ms. Armstrong kneeled down to examine Kylie's knee, which had already stopped bleeding.

Jinna looked over the teacher's head at Kylie's pouting face. *You melon-head, Kylie!* she thought.

Priscilla is my friend, and you leave her alone! She would have loved to tell Kylie off, in fluent English, but the words wouldn't come out.

The best Jinna could do was sneer at Kylie in disgust. Kylie looked shocked, but the teacher led her away before she could say anything. On her way inside, Kylie looked back at Jinna. Jinna stuck out her tongue.

That night, when her mother got home from work, Jinna was still in bed, awake.

"You're my best friend," she taught her mother to say in English—the first complete sentence Jinna had spoken in English.

"Yu ma bess fa-ren," her mother repeated, adding in Chinese, "What does it mean?"

Jinna translated, describing Priscilla in the most wonderful terms she could think of. "She's like a rainbow—no! What are those little glass things called? Like a prism," Jinna said. "When she's around, I feel like the sun is shining through me and making colors."

Mama smiled. "Good. Now you are happy in America," she said.

But Jinna still didn't feel completely happy. The busier she got with her schoolwork, the less time she spent with her Yarn People. Her imagination seemed to have run dry, and she hadn't yet figured out what kind of tests the Princess should take. In the Monkey King books, Monkey and Pigsy always seemed to be fighting, with their pointed stick and rake, against monsters and demons and ogres. Demons would have been fun to create out of yarn, but Jinna didn't want the Princess to fight. The Princess was too dignified for that.

So the game came to a halt. Week after week, Princess Jade-Blossom and Monkey King and Pigsy sat silently on Jinna's table and watched her do her homework. Often Jinna just sat there, staring at her paper, feeling dumber than dumb.

As each week went by, Jinna realized that her speaking problem was not going away. At home with Mama, she practiced new English words every day, but the minute she entered the school door, the words got trapped in her throat. Patience and understanding began to wear thin as everyone expected her to act like a normal student. Father got increasingly disappointed and angry. Mama got nervous and sad. Ms. Linden got slower and louder. Even Ms. Armstrong was frustrated.

"OK, Gina," Ms. Armstrong said to Jinna one day in February, with a note of concern in her voice, "here's your math paper, which I graded. You're very good in math! I'm proud of you."

Jinna sensed the tension in her teacher's voice and didn't look up.

"Look." Ms. Armstrong put the paper on Jinna's desk as she knelt beside her. "You got all these number problems right. That's great!" she said, pointing to the multiplication and division problems. Jinna couldn't believe what simple math fifth graders were learning. She had learned these concepts in third grade. Ms. Armstrong continued, "But I see you need some help with the word problems."

Jinna had left them all blank. English was getting easier for her to understand when someone spoke it, but she still found written English almost impossible. She'd meant to ask Auntie for help last night, but Auntie had worked late at the restaurant.

"Margie ate one third of the pecan pie," the teacher read. "Ashley ate half of the remainder. How much was left?" Her voice was so slow and loud that the other kids looked over, curious.

One third, Jinna thought. *That's so simple.* She looked at the words, trying to figure out why she hadn't been able to understand the question. Now that Ms. Armstrong had read them aloud, Jinna could see that the letter patterns matched the sounds. But last night at home, they didn't make sense. Now she wondered what Margie looked like. Was she Chinese? And what was a pecan pie?

"How much pie was left, Gina?" Ms. Armstrong's voice grew louder. Suddenly she didn't seem so pretty and caring. Jinna felt as if the teacher was pressing in on her, humiliating her in front of the whole class. Jinna noticed Kylie looking straight at her, with a smirk on her face. Jinna looked down at her hands. She had brought Pigsy to school today, and he was itching to get out of her pocket.

"Gina, are you paying attention?" Ms. Armstrong took Jinna's chin and turned it, but Jinna kept her eyes down.

Suddenly Jinna had a vivid image: *Ms. Armstrong is like a fox, and I am the rabbit. She wants to trap me and eat me up.*

"Here, I'll help you." Ms. Armstrong picked up a pencil and drew a circle, dividing it into thirds. She wrote the name "Margie" in one segment and "Ashley" in the second segment, leaving a blank for the answer in the third. "Now you can do it, I'm sure!" she said, offering her the pencil.

Everyone was looking at Jinna. It was a ridiculously easy problem. *Ms. Armstrong must think I'm a total idiot!* Jinna felt angry and defeated. But if she wrote "1/3" in the final segment now, it would look like she hadn't been able to compute the answer on her own. So instead she continued to pretend she didn't understand what the teacher was saying.

If only, she thought, Pigsy could jump out of her pocket and run around the room, distracting the fox so the rabbit could get away. She looked up, imagining this wild chase before her eyes. How could she get away?

"Henry, can you please come over here and translate?" said Ms. Armstrong.

Henry's eyes had a look of sympathy for the first time as he translated the word problem into Chinese. "The answer's one-third," he added. "Do you know how to say that in English? It will be so much easier for you if you talk."

She flashed a look of gratitude at Henry for trying to help, but something inside her head prevented her from speaking or even writing down the answer. *Over here!* shouted Pigsy, dashing across the front of the room. *Can't catch me! I'm running to Margie's house to eat the rest of the pecan pie!*

Jinna stared across the room, smiling slightly. Ms. Armstrong sighed. "Gina knows the answer, doesn't she, Henry? She's just refusing to cooperate."

Pecan pie! shouted Pigsy. *Come catch me and we'll eat the rest of the pecan pie! We'll each eat one-sixth of the pie.*

"Ms. Armstrong?" It was Kylie's voice, whining. "I'm having a problem on page two. Can you help me, please?"

The teacher sighed again. Then she picked up the pencil and wrote "1/3" on Jinna's paper. "Fractions are hard. I'll work with you more later," said Ms. Armstrong as kindly as possible, and she went off to help Kylie.

Jinna watched the fox chase after Pigsy, leaving the rabbit alone. Jinna breathed out and reached into her pocket. Pigsy seemed kind of squashed in there, but he had still been able to protect her.

CHAPTER six

ONE DAY IN MARCH, Jinna woke up with a tickle in her throat but went to school anyway. By lunchtime, her throat felt like it was on fire. She looked in the mirror in the girls' room and saw a splotch of brilliant red with white dots on it. Priscilla saw, too.

"Omigosh," said Priscilla, her eyes widening with horror. "Must be strep throat. I had it last year. It's awful. Does it hurt like heck?"

Jinna nodded.

"Like a knife cutting through your neck?" Priscilla sliced her neck with her hand, eyes in a question. Then she felt Jinna's forehead. "I don't think you have a fever. They never let you go home unless you do. But I bet you will soon. Want me to tell the teacher?"

Jinna shook her head. She could not go home. No one was there. She didn't want any special attention. She would wait till the end of the day.

Back in class, Jinna's head felt so light she had to put it down on her desk.

"Gina!" Ms. Armstrong's voice sounded worried. But Jinna didn't have the energy to lift her head.

"Gina!" Ms. Armstrong came to her desk and lifted her chin with a cool, white hand. "Is something wrong?" Jinna stared off into space. Priscilla had gone out to a special reading class, so she wasn't there to answer for Jinna.

A student teacher was helping Ms. Armstrong that day, and Ms. Armstrong asked her to watch the class while she took Jinna to the front office. Standing near the front desk was the tall, burly man with the black wire-rim glasses, the man who had kept Jinna from escaping the first day of school.

"Hello, Ron," Ms. Armstrong said when she saw him. Jinna barely had the energy to look up. She shifted her eyes to his shoes, well-worn brown loafers. "Gina, this is Mr. Caccamo. He's the school counselor," explained her teacher.

Jinna wondered if *school counselor* was another word for *principal* in America.

"Well, whom do we have here?" he asked.

"You remember Gina Zhang, don't you? " said Ms. Armstrong, mispronouncing *Zhang* as usual. "She's acting odd today. I can't tell if she's sick or upset about something. She won't make eye contact."

"Hello, Gina," the counselor said to her. "What's wrong?"

Jinna kept her eyes to the floor, but swept them across the carpet till she saw the legs of a chair. If she felt faint, she would move toward the chair. Suddenly she felt freezing cold.

"Is the nurse here today?" asked Ms. Armstrong.

"No." Mr. Caccamo knelt on one knee and spoke directly to Jinna. "Can you tell us what feels bad, Gina? Your stomach? Your head?"

His words swam together and sounded more foreign than usual. *Kinyu tailis whafees badji na? Yastahmak? Yerhay?* What was he asking her? Her throat felt on fire. When she swallowed, it threatened not to open again.

"She still doesn't speak?" Mr. Caccamo asked Ms. Armstrong.

"No," the teacher said. "I've tried everything you suggested. She hasn't said a word to anyone since the day she arrived. I think you may need to do an evaluation. It might be something more serious than we thought."

Jinna didn't get every word, but she understood enough to know that something was wrong with her. Something bad. She had suspected so all along. Now her throat was tighter than ever. It couldn't be throat cancer, could it?

Ms. Armstrong asked the secretary to call Jinna's parents, and Mr. Caccamo offered to let Jinna stay with him so her teacher could go back to their classroom. He took Jinna's hand and led her to a chair in his office. It was not a moment too soon, because if she had waited any longer, she might have fainted. The pain was so bad that Jinna couldn't concentrate on anything Mr. Caccamo was saying.

"Gina, your teacher is worried about you," said Mr. Caccamo. "Can you look at me?"

Jinna understood but did not look up. His words sounded like they were coming from underwater, and her vision was blurring. She tried to focus on a purple square on the carpet, but the soreness in her throat kept taking her mind away.

"Gina, can you understand what I'm saying?"

I want to go home, thought Jinna.

Mr. Caccamo pulled out two small plastic game pieces, one red and one green. "Point to the red one," he said.

Jinna looked up at him miserably and put her hand on her throbbing throat.

"Does your throat hurt?" he asked. The counselor came over and felt her forehead.

"You're burning up!" He poked his head out the door and spoke to the secretary. She had just reached the restaurant on the telephone and was talking to Auntie. "Yes, sick. You must come to school to get her," Jinna heard her say, slowly and clearly. "As soon as possible."

Jinna slumped back in the chair, relieved. All she could think about was the thick, pink quilt on her bed and how nice it would be to curl up in it.

When Auntie and Mama arrived, Mr. Caccamo talked to them in a low voice. "Still not speaking in school," Jinna heard him say. ". . . very concerned . . . like to meet with you and Jinna's father . . . tests . . . as soon as she is well . . . Call me . . ."

Auntie and Mama were strangely quiet as they walked Jinna home. Mama kept her arm around Jinna's shoulders, supporting her the whole way. Perhaps Jinna was imagining it, but Mama and Auntie seemed to be looking at her with new eyes, wondering what sort of serious problem had been brewing in their house without them noticing.

When she got home, she went straight to bed, and Auntie gave her some little green pills with water. Mama sat by her bed the whole night.

CHAPTER **seven**

BY MIDNIGHT, Jinna's fever had reached 102 degrees. She kicked off the pink quilt and thrashed in her bed. The next day Mama stayed at home, wiping Jinna's face with cool, wet cloths. Auntie made Jinna gargle with salt water and fed her some Chinese herbal medicine to bring the fever down.

Jinna's throat was so swollen she couldn't speak, even in Chinese, but Mama could always figure out how she was feeling. Mama made chicken soup for lunch and noodles for dinner. Jinna ate only a little.

Was her throat punishing her? Jinna wondered. Or was her body punishing her throat?

The second morning, Jinna's fever came down a little and her throat was less swollen, but it still had little white dots on it. At ten-thirty, Mama had to leave for the lunchtime shift at the restaurant. She smoothed Jinna's bangs off her forehead and wiped her face with a cool cloth before leaving.

"If you feel worse, or if you need anything, call me. You know the number," Mama said. "There's hot tea in the thermos. Drink lots of it today."

Jinna nodded. She heard the front door close and knew Mama was walking to the bus stop. After a few minutes, she slipped out of bed. The Yarn People had been clamoring for attention. She opened the drawer and pulled out the Princess, Pigsy, and the Monkey King. Then she climbed back on her bed. Monkey's home was on the pillow. The Princess stood across the way, on the quilt, talking to Pigsy.

. . . "What did Monkey King mean by tests, Pigsy?" the Princess asked.

"Oh, you know, the usual," said Pigsy, thinking about his dinner.

"Like what?"

"Oh, fighting demons, battling ogres, overcoming the mountain spirits, that sort of thing."

"Princesses don't fight."

Pigsy sat down, stumped. "Well, what do they do? I don't know much about girl things. I mean, how can you tell a princess from an ordinary girl? Is it the clothes she wears?"

The Princess laughed. How could anyone not see the difference? "Oh, Pigsy, you silly melon-head. Princesses aren't like ordinary girls at all. They're . . ." How should she say it? "Well, they are very clever and brave. And they are noble. They hold their heads high no matter what happens. Everyone admires them, and they walk among their people with grace and confidence."

"And when they are not among their people?"

"When they are in foreign lands, they are still admired. They can speak every foreign tongue with ease. They —"

"Ha! Ha! Ha!" Monkey King flew off his high rock, sailed across the lake, and landed next to the Princess and Pigsy. "I heard every word you said. So now I know."

"Know what?" The Princess was startled.

"Know what your three tests will be. You must prove you are clever, brave, and noble. Follow me, and I'll show you the first test."

The Princess did not want to go, but Pigsy convinced her she should. He picked up his rake, as if promising to defend her . . .

Jinna got out her yarn of various colors. Looking at her books, she selected a monster with two silver horns and decided to create one like him. She found some aluminum foil to make his horns. She made him black and blue, with a red face. It took a while to make him just right, but she was finished by midafternoon.

. . ."Aha!" said the Silver-Horned Monster. "If I can capture the Princess and eat her flesh, I can live forever!" He was a very wicked monster who lived deep in a cave.

Jinna thought for a minute. She decided the monster should speak English.

"Aha!" the monster said again. "I eat this girl. Then I not die!"

Jinna smiled. Yes, that sounded good.

The Princess and Pigsy walked along a ridge in the mountains, formed by her quilt. The monster suddenly jumped in front of them.

"You, girl!" he shouted in English. "Stop. I eat you!" . . .

Suddenly, Jinna heard a sound and froze. It was a tapping on her bedroom window. Was it a crow? She looked up in fear.

Priscilla's wide brown face and silly smile filled the bottom pane of the window. She waved some papers. "Hi! Are you OK? Can I come in?"

Out of habit, Jinna shoved the Yarn People under her pillow. Had Priscilla seen them? Why was Priscilla here? How had she found her house?

Jinna pointed to the back door. She went into the kitchen, still wearing her nightshirt, and unlocked the door to let her friend in.

"Omigosh, are you OK?" Priscilla asked. "I was so worried. Your throat looked so awful the other day. Have you seen a doctor? Lemme see your throat."

Jinna opened her mouth. Priscilla looked inside. "I can't see anything in this light. Does it still hurt?"

Jinna gestured with her hand, meaning "so-so."

"I brought your homework papers. I don't know if you want them or not." She handed them to Jinna.

Feeling awkward, Jinna put the papers on the kitchen table. Priscilla babbled on. "In science, we're starting to study about ecosystems, and everyone is supposed to bring a big plastic soda bottle so we can make terrariums—you know, to put dirt and plants and bugs in. Do you have one?"

Priscilla looked around the little kitchen. Jinna noticed her studying the big metal cooking wok on the stove, the bamboo steamer baskets, and the bouquet of chopsticks sticking up from the dish drainer. Jinna and her family didn't drink soda.

"It's OK," Priscilla said. "If you don't have a soda bottle, I'll bring an extra one from home. We're also supposed to get started writing our stories for Young Authors' Day. Do you know about that?"

Priscilla sat down at the kitchen table. Jinna thought Priscilla probably shouldn't be there and wondered if Mama would be coming home early today. She glanced at the clock: it was 3:15.

"Well," Priscilla continued, "it's something our school does every year, in May. Everybody in the whole school, even the kindergarten kids, has to write a story. A book, actually. They make you type it up on the computer and print it out, and then you cut the story and paste it into a book and you have to draw pictures to go with it . . . Hey!"

Still trying to make sense of Priscilla's rush of words, Jinna was startled.

"Hey, what were you playing with in your bedroom when I knocked on the window?"

Jinna's face went stony. She did not want to reveal her secret Yarn People to anyone from this new school. Not even Priscilla. It was her private world, the only place she could go to get away from everything foreign around her.

"It looked like little dolls, or something. What were they?"

Dolls! They were hardly dolls. Jinna went to the back door, opened it, and pointed out to the yard.

"What do you mean, you want me to go? Did I

say something wrong? I said something stupid, didn't I?" Her mouth kept moving even as she stood up and walked to the door. "Are the dolls a secret, or something?"

Jinna kept her face stony. *A-seek-rut,* she repeated in her mind. She thought she remembered what that word meant.

Jinna looked away. Yes, her Yarn People were a secret. She wished Priscilla hadn't seen them.

"OK, fine, be that way. Be mad, I don't care. But if you're not in school tomorrow, I'll come by again after school and bring you your homework papers, OK?" Priscilla's brown eyes were sincere. "We're best friends, right?"

Jinna hesitated, remembering how mean the other kids were to Priscilla. She nodded and half-smiled into her friend's eyes. It was enough.

"OK!" said Priscilla breezily as she swept out the door. "I hope you're feeling better!"

The third morning, Jinna did feel better. Her fever was gone, and her throat hurt only a little bit. But Mama insisted she stay at home just one more day, to make sure she was completely recovered. Jinna wondered if Priscilla would keep her promise and come after school again. Part of her wanted Priscilla to keep her nose out of Jinna's private world, but another part eagerly hoped Priscilla would care enough to come.

Mama left her alone, locking all the doors, but at noon Jinna unlocked the back door. She decided to watch the clock so she would know when Priscilla was coming.

But then her Yarn People called to her, and she got lost in their world. One of the Silver-Horned Monster's horns had fallen off, and she had to glue it on before she could begin. He was very big and hideous. Jinna was proud of him.

. . . Pigsy tried to fight with his rake, but he could not stop the Silver-Horned Monster from carrying off Princess Jade-Blossom.

"Monkey!" she called out as the Monster carried her off. "I told you I would not fight! This isn't fair!" But Monkey King was nowhere to be seen. Perhaps he had turned into a flea on the Monster's back, or a little devil in the Monster's cave, or perhaps even a rock. Who could tell with Monkey King?

The Silver-Horned Monster showed the Princess a big pot where he planned to cook her. "I not hungry now," he said in a gruff voice. "I eat you later."

He quizzed the Princess about who she was, and she answered in perfect English, or at least as good as Jinna could manage. He boasted about how he had terrorized the people in the Land of Far-Away and eaten their last queen.

The Princess didn't find him very frightening. He was such an odd-looking monster. Surely she could outsmart him. But how? She knew she had to get out of this situation before he got bored and threw her in the pot.

Then the Monster asked about the famous Monkey King, whom he'd heard of but never met.

That gave Jade-Blossom an idea. "Why eat me when you can eat Monkey King?" she asked. "You eat Monkey King, you get magic."

The Silver-Horned Monster wasn't as clever as the Princess. "Is true?"

"Oh, yes. Eat Monkey King is much better than eat me."

But the Monster was suspicious. "You stay here. You cannot go," he said.

"Not worry," said the Princess. "Monkey King come here and get me. Then you eat him. But I not tell you my a-secret."

"What a-secret?" The Monster hesitated.

"It's a-secret about Monkey King. Nobody know it but me. I not tell."

"You tell me, girl, or I eat you now!" he answered, shaking his silver horns.

"Monkey King can change shape. Is here now!"

the Princess said. "You no see him?"

The monster roared loudly, to scare her, but the Princess just laughed. "You joking me!" he shouted in his low voice. "Monkey King is not here!"

She pointed to a rock. "Monkey King turn into rock," she said. "Here is Monkey King. But Monster cannot eat rock!" She laughed a happy tee-hee-hee.

The Silver-Horned Monster grew angry, his face redder than ever. "This is lie!" he said. "Not true!"

Princess Jade-Blossom laughed and picked up the rock. "You can't get it! I have Monkey King! Na-na-na!" She ran, and the monster chased her.

"Give me rock!" the Monster shouted.

"No!" said the Princess. "Ha, ha!"

The Monster grabbed the rock from her hand. "I have Monkey King!" he said, triumphantly.

"Give back! Don't eat!" said the Princess. "Don't eat Monkey King!"

"I eat Monkey," said the Monster. "I get magic."

He stuffed the rock in his mouth, tried to chew and swallow it, and choked. "Agckkkhhh!" he cried. He jumped up, swirled, and died dramatically in the middle of Jinna's bed.

"You kill Monster!" shouted Pigsy, who appeared suddenly.

"You pass test!" shouted Monkey King, just as suddenly by his side. "Yeay! Yeay! You very clever!"

Jinna dropped the Yarn People and clapped. But when she stopped, the clapping continued.

Jinna spun around. Priscilla was standing in her bedroom doorway, clapping and smiling. "Wow! That was awesome!"

A burning anger spread over Jinna's face and neck. What right had Priscilla to sneak up on her and listen to her story? What right had Priscilla to enter her private world, to hear her secrets, to know the Monkey King or the Princess?

"I didn't know you could speak English so well, Gina. I mean, it's great!" Priscilla babbled on. "You know lots more words than I thought. I'm so glad I finally heard your voice! Why haven't you said . . ."

That did it! Priscilla was just like all the others. She wanted Jinna to talk. Priscilla didn't care if the whole school laughed at Jinna's broken English.

"No!" Jinna roared at Priscilla. "You go! You go!" Her voice cracked and her throat tightened, and no more words would come out. She stood up and lunged at Priscilla. Priscilla turned and ran, scattering the homework papers and slamming the screen door behind her. Jinna was following closely and almost ran into the door. Priscilla turned around only when she reached the side of the house.

"I just brought you your homework. No reason to be so mad!" Priscilla shouted. Then she ran off.

CHAPTER eight

THE NEXT MORNING at school, Jinna silently took her seat. She glanced across the room at Priscilla, but Priscilla didn't look up. She was rushing to finish a homework assignment.

"Gina! I'm so glad that you're feeling better," Ms. Armstrong said. "I'll tell Mr. Caccamo you're back. He's been eager to see you."

Jinna stared at the floor, imagining herself as an ant inside her desk. The pencils would look so big. But at least nobody would talk to her.

Ms. Armstrong had set aside a whole hour for the students to work on their stories for Young Authors' Day. "As fifth graders, we're the oldest in the school," she said. "Think of the stories you've written over the years. This year, your stories should be the best ever. We have a lot of work to do between now and May fourteenth."

After the other kids got out their papers or went to the computers to start writing, Ms. Armstrong came to Jinna's desk. Jinna handed her the homework papers she had completed. "Very good, Gina! Who brought these papers home to you?"

No answer.

"It was Priscilla, wasn't it? That was nice of her. Today we're writing stories." Ms. Armstrong put a blank piece of lined paper in front of Jinna. "I know this will be hard. Maybe Ms. Linden can help you. Think of a story. It's OK to write it in Chinese if you want to."

Jinna wrote her name, Gina Zhang, in neat letters at the top. Then she stopped. How could she write a story in English?

She looked around. The teacher had rearranged the desks, and Kylie sat next to her now. Kylie had already written half a page and was scribbling furiously. Curious, Jinna started to read what Kylie had written. Handwriting was harder to read than printed words, but the story seemed to be about two girls trying to find a missing dog.

Suddenly Kylie noticed Jinna reading over her

shoulder. She covered her paper and snarled at Jinna, "You're reading my story, aren't you? I thought you couldn't read English. You better not copy!"

Jinna looked back at the blank paper in front of her. Kylie snatched the paper away from her. Kylie's pencil hovered over it for only a few seconds before she scratched in big letters: "BLANK PAPER, BLANK MIND." She shoved it back on Jinna's desk and then turned away, giggling.

At recess, Priscilla was as friendly as ever to Jinna, as if she'd forgotten about Jinna being mad. Jinna showed her the paper, and Priscilla blew up.

"That's awful! Kylie wrote this, didn't she? That loser," said Priscilla. "I told you she was no good. Blank mind! As if she was the smartest in the class. She's not, you know. Last year we had a different teacher, and Kylie wasn't the teacher's pet. Not by a long shot. And in third grade Kylie had to be in the special reading class with me. She's no genius. Once she even misspelled her own name. Dumb!" Priscilla hit her forehead with her palm, knocked her head back, and laughed that high-pitched laugh Jinna liked so much.

Priscilla usually said whatever came into her head, but on this day she seemed as if she was trying to be careful. Jinna was relieved. Priscilla didn't tell anyone she had been to Jinna's house or heard her voice.

Priscilla mostly talked about the same old things. But halfway through recess, Priscilla stopped jabbering and looked thoughtful. "Will you promise me something?" she asked in a soft voice. "Will you be my friend no matter how much English you learn?"

Jinna thought it was a strange request, but she nodded. *Of course I will,* she thought. *Just promise me you'll never ask about my Yarn People. It's a-secret.*

Priscilla seemed relieved. "What are you going to do about your Young Authors' story?" she asked. They were sitting by the wall near the edge of the playground, and Priscilla was arranging little stones in piles. Jinna shrugged. Her jacket rustled. None of the other students was wearing a jacket, but fifty-five degrees still felt cold to Jinna.

"Ms. Armstrong shouldn't make you write a story, since you can't speak English yet." Priscilla looked at her sideways.

Jinna said nothing.

"I promise not to tell her you can speak English. No one should know!" Priscilla seemed to be pleading with her about something, but Jinna couldn't figure out what.

"But, ya know, I was thinking . . . it's too bad. Because you could probably think up a great story."

Jinna looked away and watched a girl kick a soccer ball across the field. She tried to block out

Priscilla's words, to pretend she didn't understand. As usual, that was the cue for Priscilla to keep talking.

"I wish I could think up stories like you. My mind is like one big blank."

Jinna tried to imagine Priscilla's mind looking like blank paper.

"I've always hated Young Authors' Day. I mean, it's really stupid. Like every kid in the school could be an author someday. Yeah, right. Well, maybe some people can, but I can't. You should see how dumb my stories are. I can never think of good ideas. One year, I just wrote about our family's trip to Disneyland. You know, like how we went on the Teacups, we ate cotton candy, I threw up after the roller coaster ride, my cat ripped up the curtains while we were gone. Stupid stuff. Even *I* didn't like my story. I threw it away."

The bell rang. Recess was over. The girls stood up, but Priscilla kept talking. She didn't seem to be aware of all the other kids around them now, returning to class. She got less careful with her words.

"You have a great story already," she said. "Just do that one about the pink girl and the Monkey God, or whatever. Did you make that up or did you get it from somewhere? It sounded like you were making it up. You could just write it up and you're done!"

There it was! Priscilla had stepped over the line,

talking about her story here at school. Jinna's heart froze with fear. Did Priscilla forget she had promised to keep it a secret? Did she think no one could hear?

"The part about the rock, that was so smart . . ."

Either way, Jinna had to get her to stop talking— somehow, anyhow. She plowed into Priscilla's back, knocking her into the side of the door just as they were walking through it. Priscilla hit her shoulder on the doorjamb.

"Ouch! Quit it! Who was that?" Priscilla turned around.

"It was your *best friend.* GINA," jeered Kylie, who was right behind them. "Looks like you've made *her* mad, too. Oh, well! That's the end of that!" Kylie tossed her wavy hair and walked by with her nose in the air.

Priscilla shot Jinna a hurt look, rubbing her shoulder. Jinna hadn't meant to injure her. She had just wanted to stop Priscilla from saying anything more about the Princess. How else could Jinna have done that?

"I said something stupid, didn't I?" whispered Priscilla. Jinna felt bad about hurting her feelings, but she was upset and angry. How could Priscilla speak of the Princess at school? Didn't she realize how Jinna would feel if other people found out?

★   ★   ★

Priscilla lived in the other direction from school, so she and Jinna never walked home together. Jinna usually walked the six blocks to her house and let herself in with a key, then did her homework and heated up some leftover restaurant food till Mama got home. No one ever walked with Jinna, since she never had anything to say, and that was fine with her.

But today, when school was over, Priscilla started walking along with Jinna. Jinna sped up and looked the other way. She was still angry, and she wanted to make sure Priscilla got the message never to speak of the Princess at school. How could she get that message across without using words?

"Gina, slow down. Can I walk with you?" Priscilla said, panting a bit to catch up with her. "Seriously, I gotta talk to you, OK?"

Jinna kept walking. A light drizzle filled the air, and she watched the sidewalk for puddles. What if she were a tiny person who could float on a leaf in a puddle?

"Please don't do this to me," Priscilla pleaded. "Stop." She gently touched Jinna's arm, and Jinna stopped.

"Did I ever tell you about Michelle Eng?" Priscilla asked in a soft voice, looking around to make sure no other kids would hear. They began walking again, slowly, toward Jinna's house. "I never told you. Why would I tell you? Well, I'm telling you now. If it happens again, I'll die."

Jinna had no idea what Priscilla was talking about. But she was willing to listen.

Priscilla let out a big sigh and began. "Well, last year . . . Maybe I should start before that. Before last year, I never had any friends at all. Zero. Zip. Nada." She made a big zero with her fingers and looked at Jinna through it. Jinna didn't laugh.

"So, see, last year was different. At the beginning of the year, our class had two new girls, Sheliya and Michelle. Sheliya was friendly to everybody, including me, because she didn't know everybody hated me. Even when she figured it out, she still talked to me and acted nice. Not like the other girls. And Michelle, well, Michelle didn't speak English. Maybe a few words, like 'Hello. My name is Michelle,' but basically nothing. She just stood in the corner at recess looking lonely, so one day I started to talk to her. She seemed really happy to have a friend, and I was happy, too. You know, kind of like you and me." Priscilla glanced shyly at Jinna, who nodded.

"So Sheliya and Michelle and me starting hanging out together at recess, you know, like real friends. It was awesome! We were like a new group, and I was at the center of it. They always waited for me, and we always ate lunch together. Every day." Priscilla's smile spread across her face and she shook her head, as if she couldn't believe it. "We even had a club called the 'Cool Chicks.' Sheliya thought up that name."

She paused for a reaction from Jinna, who smiled and acted as though she knew what cold chicken had to do with it.

"Then, one day at recess . . ." Priscilla's voice grew softer. "Kylie came over and asked Sheliya to play tetherball. Sheliya was really happy, because everyone likes Kylie, see, and no one likes me. So Sheliya smiled at Michelle and me and said 'Come on, let's go!' But Kylie said, 'No, just you, Sheliya. We have teams. We just need one person.' So Sheliya went and played with Kylie and her friends." Priscilla's voice grew very sad.

"I kept thinking she would come back, but she didn't. Michelle seemed different after that. She kept getting mad at me. She said I said dumb things. I always say dumb things, and then people don't like me anymore."

Jinna saw the sadness in Priscilla's eyes. She felt mad at Kylie, mad at Sheliya, and mad at Michelle. How could they treat Priscilla that way?

The two girls had arrived at Jinna's house. Jinna stood awkwardly on the crack where the front walkway met the sidewalk.

"Can I come in? I promise to go home after I finish telling you this." Priscilla's eyes pleaded.

Jinna nodded and started up the walkway. It didn't feel as strange as she expected, unlocking the door and letting Priscilla in. They headed for the kitchen, with Priscilla talking the whole way.

"So anyway, one day Michelle and I had a big fight. She yelled at me and said I wasn't a 'Cool Chick' at all. She said I was a 'Dumb Cluck' and she didn't want me to be her friend. Sheliya came over and tried to make it better, but she couldn't. Finally, Michelle went away with Sheliya and played with Kylie and those other girls. Now Michelle doesn't talk to me."

Priscilla stood in the middle of Jinna's kitchen, hanging her head. "So I like you, 'cause you listen to me when I talk, and you don't ever say anything mean. We don't ever argue, except today you got mad at me, and now I'm so scared. I just know once you start speaking English you'll go play with those other girls. They never say anything dumb."

That's one advantage of not speaking, thought Jinna. *I never say anything dumb.* It hadn't occurred to her that other kids, American kids who spoke perfect English, could be frightened and lonely, too. What would Priscilla do if Jinna didn't sit with her anymore? Jinna had never thought about that. What would Jinna do if Priscilla didn't sit with her?

Jinna opened the refrigerator and took out two small yellow plastic bottles labeled Yakult. It was a kind of sweet yogurt drink, Jinna's favorite. She handed one to Priscilla and sat down, peeling the red foil lid off her Yakult and taking a drink.

Priscilla sat down, too, peeling the lid off hers and trying it. "It's good. I never had it before," she said. "Is it fattening?"

Jinna shrugged her shoulders and took another sip. What did this mean, *fattening?*

"You don't have to be my friend," Priscilla said, tracing her finger on the tablecloth pattern. "I just wanted you to know how I feel. I won't come over anymore if you don't want me to." She looked up.

Jinna didn't know what to do. Smiling and nodding seemed insufficient.

"I'll go now if you want me to," said Priscilla.

Jinna stared at her Yakult bottle, wondering what she could do to reassure Priscilla. She was the only friend Jinna had, and Jinna loved to listen to her talk. She had always thought Priscilla sounded so confident. Today, Priscilla seemed more like her, scared and uncertain.

Jinna wasn't sure why she did what she did next. But she stood up and walked into her bedroom, gesturing for Priscilla to follow. Jinna sat down on the floor, and so did Priscilla, looking overly large in the tiny room.

Jinna hesitated, then opened the drawer with the Yarn People in it. She took out a handful of them. *"Mao-xian ren."* Jinna said the Chinese word for Yarn People so softly it was almost a whisper.

"Maow-sen-ren," Priscilla mimicked, getting it almost right.

"Zhu Ba-jie," Jinna said, holding the pig.

Priscilla took Pigsy gently and repeated his Chinese name, "Joo Bah-jeh."

Jinna held up the Monkey King, saying *"Houzi Wang."* Her voice cracked, and she had to repeat the name to make it clear.

"Ho-zuh Wong," Priscilla said, pronouncing *Wang* the proper way. "Monkey King, right?"

Jinna smiled and nodded. She hesitated again and then reached for Princess Jade-Blossom, in her gown of pink, handmade by Yinglan. *"Gong-zhu,"* she said, adding in English, "daughter of king."

"Oh! *Princess!*" said Priscilla, teaching Jinna an important new word without realizing it. "Of course she's a princess. Are these two good guys?" she asked, holding out Pigsy and Monkey King.

Jinna nodded. *Good guys.* Well, that was one way to describe them. Anyway, they weren't the bad guys. She stood Monkey King high up on the mountain of her bed. "I am Sun Wukong, Mung-kee Keeng," she said in English, in Monkey King's voice. Monkey King could speak every language on earth.

Priscilla picked up a yarn lady with a blue dress and looked at Jinna for approval. Jinna nodded.

"I am . . . uh . . . I am Dorothy, from Kansas, and I am lost," Priscilla said in a high-pitched voice. She had never made up stories of her own. "I want to meet the Princess."

"Oh, Princess very busy. She doing test."

"I don't get it," Priscilla said in her regular voice, to Jinna. "Why is the Princess taking a test?"

Jinna refused to speak directly to her. She pointed to the blue girl and Monkey King, who spoke again. "You, girl! Speak to Monkey King. I tell story."

"OK, I wanna hear the story," Priscilla said, using the high-pitched voice.

Monkey King told the story from the beginning, about how the Princess was picked up by a crow and taken to a distant land. Jinna used the Crow and Princess to act out the story, speaking in English but in the voice of Monkey King, talking to Dorothy.

She had just introduced the idea of the three tests when suddenly Priscilla looked at her watch.

"Omigosh!" Priscilla said in her regular voice. "It's nearly five-thirty. My mother gets home from work at five o'clock, and she'll be having a heart attack around now. She'll think I've been kidnapped or run over by a truck! I better go right away. She's gonna kill me." She placed the blue yarn doll on Jinna's bed and stood up. "Bye, Gina! I gotta go. Sorry."

Jinna stood, too, suddenly feeling scared and uncertain. What if she had made a mistake, showing Priscilla her Yarn People?

"Wait," Jinna tried to say, but the word wouldn't come out. She could only mouth it. Priscilla saw her, though, and waited. "A-secret. OK?" Jinna's words were barely loud enough to hear. She held up Pigsy.

Priscilla understood. With one hand on the door-knob, she looked back at Jinna and said, "OK. It's a secret. I promise not to tell anybody about your Yarn People. You won't say anything about Michelle and Sheliya?"

Jinna shook her head no and smiled. Priscilla understood. Jinna offered Priscilla her pinkie finger.

Priscilla knew just what to do to make a "pinkie promise." She hooked her pinkie around Jinna's and squeezed. "Thanks, Gina," she whispered. "It was really fun."

CHAPTER **nine**

THE NEXT DAY, Priscilla invited Jinna to come over to her house after school, but Jinna vigorously shook her head no. New settings and someone else's parents—it was too much.

"Well, can I go to your house again sometime?"

Jinna thought for a minute, then nodded slowly. It had been fun with Priscilla the day before, and it was a relief to be able to talk to someone. Still, what if Priscilla told someone about her secret world? Priscilla couldn't possibly understand why it was so important for Jinna to have something that was hers alone, a world where she was in charge.

That evening, she told Mama about Priscilla and

asked if Priscilla could come over some afternoon. Mama thought it was not a good idea, having strangers in the house when Jinna was alone—It wasn't safe. But Jinna knew it was safe, and when Priscilla asked a week later if she could come over after school, Jinna nodded.

"Did your mom say it was OK?"

Jinna didn't nod.

"Your mom doesn't know?"

Jinna shot her a worried glance.

"I won't tell."

Jinna smiled. Priscilla always understood her, even if Jinna didn't always understand Priscilla.

Jinna and Priscilla sat in the kitchen for a long time. Priscilla didn't seem to mind. She had called her mom and told her she'd be home by five-thirty. She chatted away as usual, talking about her little brother, who was learning to stand on his head.

Jinna only half-listened. She was busy trying to figure out what the Princess's second test should be. Now that the Princess had proved she was clever, she had to prove she was brave. And Jinna didn't want the test to be just another monster in a cave. She tried to remember the various ogres and demons she had read about but decided that was too similar. How else do you prove you're brave? An idea began to form in her head. Would Priscilla think it was dumb?

bookshelf so she could hear better. Would Priscilla give away their secret? Jinna held her breath.

"You mean at school, right?" Priscilla's voice sounded shaky.

"Of course."

"No. She doesn't speak English yet." There was a pause. "She's from China," Priscilla added, as if Mr. Caccamo did not know this.

"What about at home? Does she speak at home?"

"I don't know," Priscilla lied. "I've never heard her speak English."

Jinna started breathing again, quietly.

"How much of what she hears in English does she understand?"

Priscilla hesitated. "I don't know. How would I know?" she said.

"So how can you two be friends? Does she talk to you when there aren't grownups around?"

"No!" Priscilla sounded scared. "She doesn't speak English! She can't talk! OK? I talk to her, that's all. I don't know if she understands me or not! But she's learning English in ESL class!"

"Of course she is," Mr. Caccamo said in a soothing voice. "Thanks, Priscilla. It's nice of you to be friendly to her. I'm sure she appreciates it."

Jinna waited until Priscilla walked past her toward the cafeteria and Mr. Caccamo was out of sight.

Then she ran to catch up to Priscilla. Jinna found her at the end of the lunch line.

"Hey, where were you?" Priscilla asked. "Never mind, it doesn't matter." Then she lowered her voice. "Be careful of Mr. Caccamo. If he decides there's something wrong with you, he can put you in the Special Needs class."

Jinna shot a questioning look at her.

"Special Needs class," Priscilla repeated. "Some of the kids in it are really nice. In fact, my brother's in it, with the first graders, because he's hyperactive—you know, Attention Deficit Disorder. My brother's not a bad kid, but he acts kinda wild sometimes. But they also put the real bad kids in that class. You get to stay in your regular class in the morning, but you have to go to the Special Needs classroom every afternoon. I don't know what they do there, but it's always loud when you go past their door."

Jinna looked at Priscilla with alarm.

"Don't worry," Priscilla continued in a whisper. "I won't tell them you can speak. Just pretend that you're still learning, and they'll leave you alone. No problem."

No prah-blem, Jinna thought, translating it into Chinese in her head. That was a good one to remember to teach Mama. *No prah-blem.* But something about the way Priscilla spoke worried her. Special

Needs class. She had not heard of that before. Was it a way of punishing kids who didn't cooperate?

After lunch on Wednesday, Mr. Caccamo asked Jinna to come to his office. *Here it comes,* she thought. *Is he going to punish me?* When she walked in, Jinna saw a Chinese lady wearing a lot of eye makeup and a red sweater with gold buttons. Jinna thought she had seen this lady before, eating in her uncle's restaurant.

"Gina, this is Mrs. Kwok," Mr. Caccamo said in a kind voice. "She speaks Mandarin."

"How are you, Gina?" Mrs. Kwok said in Mandarin, with a heavy Cantonese accent. "I have come here to help. This gentleman wants to ask you some questions."

Jinna nodded at the lady and sat down.

What can I do? Are they going to put me in class with those bad kids? thought Jinna. She shoved her hand in her pocket and held the Princess, trying to feel her cleverness and bravery.

"You don't have to answer in words. Just nod your head, yes or no," Mr. Caccamo said. Mrs. Kwok translated for Jinna. How could she know that Jinna understood almost everything Mr. Caccamo said?

"Gina, we're very concerned about you," he continued. "Ms. Linden says you still don't even speak in ESL class. We can't tell how much you're learning and how we should teach you." Mr. Caccamo's eyebrows were very thick and bushy, and Jinna watched how they jumped as he spoke. They looked alive.

Mrs. Kwok translated into Chinese. She seemed very distant and cold.

"Do you understand people when they speak in English?" Mr. Caccamo asked.

Jinna understood the question perfectly and tried to think of a good answer as she waited for Mrs. Kwok to translate. Sometimes Jinna understood, and sometimes she didn't. It depended how hard the words were. But how do you answer that with a yes-or-no nod of the head? And what was the right answer? What was he expecting her to say?

Jinna shrugged her shoulders and looked at the floor.

"Do you have any trouble speaking at home, in Chinese?" he asked.

Mrs. Kwok translated.

Jinna shook her head. *Wonder what he would look like as a Yarn Person,* she thought. *How would I make those eyebrows?*

"Are you afraid of making a mistake in English? You shouldn't be. Everyone makes mistakes at first."

Mr. Caccamo pulled out a list of questions and began asking them. Jinna knew that he was trying to figure out a way to solve her problem. But he didn't realize he was making her feel worse. She tried to block out the words by staring at Mr. Caccamo's desktop. She saw a bright-colored rock there with two goldfish painted on it. She had an image of shoving it into his mouth, to get him to stop talking.

Why couldn't he just leave her alone? In China, she had seldom spoken in class, and no one made her feel as if she had some psychological defect. Why did this man have to make Jinna feel even stranger and more out of place than she already felt in this new country?

The more questions Mr. Caccamo asked, the more stubborn Jinna got. Most of the questions assumed she was very stupid and had not learned anything. As far as she could tell, he was judging her. He was humiliating her. Her throat wouldn't let her answer, but she also didn't *want* to answer. She shouldn't *have* to answer. So she didn't. She barely moved her head up or down or sideways. Even Mrs. Kwok was frustrated by the end.

Finally Mrs. Kwok turned to Jinna and said, "I have a son in the sixth grade. He was in third grade when we moved to America, and he had no trouble learning English. In fact, by the end of the first year, he was third in his class." She had an accusing look in her eyes, as if she thought Jinna was making all

Chinese immigrants look bad. "Most Chinese children are very smart and can say a lot of words after a few months. I don't know why you are having so much trouble."

Jinna began counting squares on the rug and trying to make up a story about the little purple and red people who might live there.

Mr. Caccamo asked Mrs. Kwok to tell him what she had just said to Jinna. When Mrs. Kwok did, he turned red and said, "That's not the way I would put it." There was a sharp edge to his voice. "Please tell Gina this instead. Lots of kids come here not knowing English at all. They learn to speak eventually. I'm sure Gina will, too."

Jinna felt flushed. She wished she could look straight at him and say, "Listen, Mister, if I could speak in school, I would. But I can't, OK? So leave me alone. I'm doing the best I can. Please stop treating me like I'm some kind of an oddball."

Jinna focused her eyes on the soft squares on the rug. Were the squares actually jails? Maybe the little people died when they were boxed in there.

Mrs. Kwok repeated what Mr. Caccamo had said. When Jinna looked away, Mrs. Kwok sighed and shook her head. "I've never seen a case like this," she said in English. "I hope you can help her."

CHAPTER **ten**

THAT NIGHT, Mr. Caccamo called Jinna's parents. He asked them to come to his office for a conference Friday after school. When Jinna heard this, her throat closed up so much it almost choked her.

"You told me you would speak at school!" Father shouted.

Jinna looked away. Of course she had told him that. What else could she tell him?

"She's really trying," said Mama.

"She doesn't speak at all?"

"A little, I think," said Mama. "Just not enough."

"Now it sounds like she's in trouble. That man

said we have to go meet him. What's wrong with you?" Her father's eyes looked both miserable and angry. Jinna's heart sank.

Just before lunch on Thursday, Mr. Caccamo came to Jinna's classroom and asked to speak to Priscilla, Kylie, Sheliya, and Jinna.

"Girls," he said, smiling, "I'd like to invite the four of you to have lunch with me today. Go ahead and get your lunches and bring them back to my office."

None of the other girls seemed alarmed by this. Priscilla said she had eaten lunch with Mr. Caccamo several times before. He tried to meet with all the kids in small groups during the year. He called it "lunch bunch." Last year, he had made her eat lunch with Kylie after the big fiasco with Michelle and Sheliya. Today Michelle was absent, or she probably would have been invited, too.

But Jinna was suspicious. After the meeting with Mr. Caccamo and Mrs. Kwok, she was sure it had something to do with her.

Still, what could she do? She followed Sheliya and Priscilla into Mr. Caccamo's office. Kylie was already there, eating carrots and yogurt she'd brought from home. Jinna pulled out the lunch Mama had packed—a plastic container with some leftover restaurant food. Today it was fish head stew.

"Gross! What's that horrible smell?" asked Kylie when Jinna lifted the lid of her container. "Yuck. I can't believe she eats that stuff," Kylie whispered to Sheliya.

Mr. Caccamo tried to put the girls at ease, talking casually about things going on at school. He even played soft, soothing music in the background as the five of them ate their lunches.

"So, what projects have you been working on in class?" he asked.

"Terrariums." Kylie jumped in first. "Sheliya and I are partners. Ours is the best. We have lots of plants growing, and three sow bugs. They are so cute!"

"My sow bug died," said Priscilla. "We had to take them out to count their legs, and I squished him."

"Who is your partner, Priscilla?" Mr. Caccamo asked.

"Gina. She counted the legs on hers—fourteen, right?" Priscilla asked. Jinna nodded. "She didn't squish hers. We named it Sally."

"We had a spelling test with words like *isopod* and *ecosystem*," said Sheliya. "I studied really hard and only missed two."

"It was the hardest test all year, and I got them all right!" said Kylie.

Jinna couldn't eat a bite of her lunch, so she sipped her chocolate milk and listened. She checked the window for crows. She examined the bright butterfly clips in Kylie's wavy hair. She tried to count Sheliya's braids.

"Are there many new kids in your class this year?" Mr. Caccamo asked.

"Not too many," said Priscilla. "Only about six or eight." She began naming the new kids, and Sheliya and Kylie chimed in, too.

"Also Gina," added Mr. Caccamo.

"Oh, yeah, of course," said Kylie. "It's easy to forget about her because she doesn't talk—yet."

Jinna noticed that Mr. Caccamo had a pen set on his desk that was collecting dust. Obviously, he never used it.

"Do you think she would talk if she felt more comfortable?" he asked.

"Oh, no, she can't speak English," said Kylie.

"I think she's just shy," said Sheliya, looking at Jinna in a curious but friendly way. "I wonder what her voice sounds like."

Priscilla shifted in her seat, looking like she was about to burst. Jinna hoped Priscilla would be able to resist the urge to blurt out everything she knew.

"I feel sorry for her," said Kylie, but Jinna knew she was just trying to impress Mr. Caccamo. "I sit next to her now. We're all working hard to finish our stories for Young Authors' Day, and Gina just sits there, staring at her paper. She'll never be able to write a story."

"Maybe not this year," said Sheliya. "Michelle couldn't write one last year, remember? But she's doing one this year. It just takes time."

"You guys have no idea!" Priscilla erupted. "Gina is so smart, you wouldn't believe! She is really good at making up stories. She thinks of all kinds of interesting people, and places, and everything. She has a great imagination. She'd write the best story of all if she could write in English."

For a moment, everyone was silent, staring at Priscilla. *She's standing up for me. She wants them to know I'm not an idiot,* thought Jinna. *But if she tells them about my Yarn People, I'll just die.*

"You're the one with the great imagination if you think Gina can make up stories when she can't even talk," said Kylie with scorn.

"Have you heard her talk, Priscilla?" Mr. Caccamo zoomed in on her.

"No! Of course I haven't." Priscilla had backed herself into a corner. "She can't speak English."

"Then how do you know that she can tell stories?" Mr. Caccamo kept his voice soft and gentle.

Three pairs of eyes bored into Priscilla. *As long as she doesn't mention the Yarn People, maybe it's OK for her to tell them I can speak,* thought Jinna. *Of course,*

Priscilla probably won't because she doesn't want Kylie or Sheliya to know. "I tell you, she's really smart. She's gonna show you someday," Priscilla finally said.

"That's nice of you to stand up for her, Priscilla," said Mr. Caccamo. "That's a sign of friendship. We need to assume that everyone does their best work. What other signs of friendship do you notice in your classmates?"

Jinna and Priscilla began breathing again. They didn't dare look at each other. Mr. Caccamo went on about friends and friendship. Kylie responded with all the right answers, and Sheliya occasionally jumped in. Priscilla remained unusually silent, concentrating on finishing her lunch.

When lunch period was over, Mr. Caccamo thanked the girls for joining him. As they were walking back to class, Kylie came up next to Priscilla. "What did you mean about Gina telling stories?" Kylie asked. "Have you really heard her talk?"

"You go away, Kylie Anderson!" Priscilla hissed. "You mind your own business."

"Once Gina starts talking," Kylie pressed on, "Sheliya and I will ask her to sit with us at lunch."

"I hate you, Kylie!" said Priscilla.

"Oh, you've hurt my feelings," snapped Kylie, sarcastically. "I'm going to tell Mr. Caccamo you're not being a good friend."

★ ★ ★

. . . The Princess never cried, even when she was lonely. One day, some young ladies from the Land of Far-Away invited her to have tea at a teahouse high on the hill. Dorothy did not come, but three other young ladies did, dressed in red, yellow, and purple. They all had pretty skirts, though not as nice as Jade-Blossom's.

"Tell me a little about Far-Away," she said to one of them, pouring a cup of tea. "Do the girls here learn embroidery and music?"

"Oh, no," said the young lady dressed in purple. "We all prefer soccer and softball."

"We have great television programs here," said the young lady in red, taking a sip of her tea, the finest Long-jing tea. "Do you want some sugar?"

The Princess ignored her question. No one puts sugar in fine Chinese tea. "When you were in school, did you memorize Tang poetry?" she asked instead, feeling out of place.

"Sometimes we memorized poems," said the young lady dressed in yellow. "But mostly we read Baby Sitters Club books."

"Ah, baby-sitting. I used to look after my younger brothers and sisters at the palace," said the Princess. "Do you like to baby-sit?"

The young ladies exchanged looks, as if they all

knew something she didn't know. "What about you?" asked the one in purple. "At the palace, what do you do for fun?"

"Sometimes I swing or fly kites or walk in the garden," said the Princess.

"You're making this up, aren't you? Are you really a princess?" asked the red lady, with an odd smile.

"Of course I am!" Jade-Blossom was offended. "Why would you doubt it?"

"Look at your skirt," said the yellow one. The edge of the Princess's beautiful pink skirt had gotten wet when she rescued Dorothy, and now it looked ragged. "I thought princesses always wore beautiful clothes and had magic powers."

"Do you have magic powers?" asked the young lady in purple. "Will you show us?"

"A princess never uses her magic just to prove something," said the Princess. She wasn't about to tell the young ladies that her powers had gone. She poured a second round of tea from the same tea leaves, feeling nervous.

The young ladies began whispering, and Jade-Blossom tried to ignore them. But after a short time, they left. The Princess felt troubled.

An hour later, two soldiers showed up at the door.

"We have come to take you in for questioning," one soldier said. "Follow us."

"Pigsy! Monkey King!" she called out. "Why am I being arrested? I'm supposed to face the third test now." But the soldiers grabbed her and dragged her down the hill from the teahouse. "What did I do wrong? It's not fair!" she cried.

In the town square, hundreds of people were standing around, jabbering in loud voices. The soldiers took her up to a platform where everybody could see her.

I am a true princess, thought Jade-Blossom. *I have nothing to fear.* But the sight of all those hundreds of faces made her quake inside. She wished she could call up her old magic powers and fly away, but the soldiers were gripping her arms tightly.

From the platform, she could see the young ladies in the front row: yellow, red, and purple. The yellow one was laughing and pointing at her.

"Why have you done this to me?" the Princess said angrily.

"It was a test of your magic powers," said the girl in purple. "We wanted to see you use them."

"If you were a princess, you would have flown away," taunted the young lady in yellow. "But obviously, you are not what you say you are." . . .

CHAPTER **eleven**

BY FRIDAY AFTERNOON, Jinna was dreading the meeting with her parents and Mr. Caccamo, who insisted she be present. He had a long table in his office, and he seated her at it when she arrived. Soon Ms. Linden came in, and then Ms. Armstrong, each with a folder of material about Jinna. Another teacher came in, too, one Jinna had never seen before. She had alarmingly curly red hair.

Jinna noticed Mrs. Kwok wasn't there. She wondered why Mr. Caccamo hadn't asked her to come.

The teachers and Mr. Caccamo sat on the far side of the table, facing Jinna. Next to her were three empty chairs left for her parents and aunt. When everyone had arrived and sat down, they looked like the Zhangs vs. Hilltop School. Jinna felt as if she were on trial. She had a sinking feeling she already knew what the judgment would be.

"If we use any English words you're unfamiliar with, please ask us to explain," Mr. Caccamo began. "We're very concerned about Gina."

Auntie translated for Mama and Father. "They have a concept about Jinna," she said. Although Jinna had been in America only four months, she realized that she understood Mr. Caccamo and her teachers far better than Auntie did.

Ms. Linden spoke first. She described how Jinna acted in ESL class. In her opinion, Jinna just needed more time to learn English. Ms. Linden had seen silent children before, and the condition usually went away as children got more comfortable in their environment.

"This teacher lady says Jinna will learn English just fine," translated Auntie. Father and Mama both seemed relieved.

Then Ms. Armstrong spoke. She had done some research and found out that some children refuse to speak in order to get attention and to manipulate their teachers. "Of course, I don't think Gina is doing this, but I think you should know that some children do. We need to watch out."

"This teacher lady says Jinna is a bad girl and doing this on purpose," Auntie translated.

Jinna felt miserable. Which teacher would they believe?

Mr. Caccamo said he had tried to do an evaluation of Jinna but found it difficult, since she did not respond. The school had a special program that could help her, but first he needed to have her parents answer some questions.

"This man says he cannot put a value on Jinna because she doesn't talk to him," Auntie translated. "But maybe she can watch some programs. First, he wants to ask you questions."

Jinna shook her head at Auntie's translation. She wished she could jump in and translate his real meaning.

Mr. Caccamo had a written list of questions. "First of all, does Gina have any trouble speaking at home—in Chinese?"

Jinna wished she were not there. She tried to escape the room by calling up an image she liked: a grassy field with little girls running around catching butterflies. But the image kept slipping out of focus, and the channel kept switching back to the tension in Mr. Caccamo's office.

Auntie started to answer the question herself, but Mr. Caccamo insisted Jinna's parents answer. Mama remained silent while Father tried to answer in broken English. Finally he had to let Auntie translate for him.

"She speaks just fine at home," he said. "She's perfectly normal."

There! thought Jinna. *Now they know. Let's go home.* But it wouldn't be that easy, she knew.

"Did she have any trouble speaking at school in China?"

"No trouble at all."

Jinna squirmed. That wasn't exactly true. Father knew she had mostly stopped speaking after the Little Raindrop incident, but apparently he didn't want the American schoolteachers to know.

"Have you noticed any hearing problems?"

Father looked at Jinna with surprise. "No, I don't think so."

"In China, did she take any standardized tests?"

Auntie had trouble translating that one.

"Was she learning at grade level?"

Auntie couldn't figure out that question either.

"Was she a good student?"

"Oh yes, very good. Very good girl at school. Never talking very much." Auntie began to add in a few of her own opinions.

"What does she tell you about school here? Does she like school?"

Father looked at Mama. Jinna knew it had never occurred to them to ask her if she liked school. In China, it didn't matter what children thought of the school. Only the parents' opinions counted for anything, and they would never insult or contradict teachers. "Of course we like school very much. We like America."

Mr. Caccamo asked a lot of other questions, too, such as: When Gina was small, was she afraid of people? Did she start speaking late? Had she experienced any trauma as a small child? Did any other family members have a problem speaking in public places? Jinna could tell that Father was anxious about being asked these questions. Family matters are usually private in China, and when public officials start asking personal questions, it usually means trouble.

"She's been at Hilltop for more than four months now. Has she told you why she doesn't speak?"

"She speaks sometimes. Just not very much," said Father through Auntie.

"No," said Mr. Caccamo. "No one at our school has ever heard Gina's voice at all, in any language."

Father had a brief, heated exchange with Mama. "You told me she speaks sometimes!" he hissed.

"I thought she did," said Mama, weakly.

Father turned to Jinna. "This man says you don't speak at all in school! Is this true?"

Jinna nodded. *Princess! Monkey King! Butterflies! Carpet-square people!* Why wouldn't some image come into her head and take her away from here?

"You speak now and show him you can speak. Now!" Father stared at her.

She stared back, miserably silent.

"Speak in Chinese or English, either one. Say these words: 'I can speak. No problem.'"

Seven pairs of eyes focused on her, all the important adults in her life.

I can speak, no problem, thought Jinna. *I can speak at home, with Mama and Auntie. I can speak with Priscilla, although you don't know that. I can even speak English. But if you think I can speak now, with all of you grownups looking at me, you're wrong.*

Still, she had to try. She opened her mouth to speak. Everyone watched her closely. The metal band tightened around her neck and she felt an almost physical pain. *I . . .* The word sat at the back of her throat, but her voice box would not push it out. Perhaps if they would all stop staring at her, she could say the words they were waiting to hear: *I can speak. Please don't worry about me. Just leave me alone. I am learning fast, so fast! I'll be fluent someday, just you wait! You'll see!*

But no words came out of her mouth. Father pushed his chair back and stood up, towering over

Jinna and speaking in a loud whisper. "These people think you are stupid," he said in Chinese. "They think you are not normal. Open your mouth right now and tell them you can speak just fine. There is no problem."

These people think I am stupid. They think I am not normal. The words rang in Jinna's ears. She looked down at the table. The fish rock was in the middle of the table. She wanted to pick it up and throw it through the window. Why hadn't she been able to talk, when it mattered the most?

"Jinna, please." It was Mama. "Just say a word or two in Chinese, so they will know you are normal." Her eyes were pleading.

Jinna shook her head in embarrassment. The words "I can speak" had died in her throat. Maybe she wasn't normal. Maybe there really was something wrong.

Father looked at Mr. Caccamo. "She hasn't spoken at all since November?" he asked, speaking in Chinese and letting Auntie translate.

"No."

"Why didn't you tell us earlier?"

"We thought you knew."

"She promised me she would speak. She can speak. She should speak. I want her to speak. I told her to speak. Can you fix this problem?"

Mr. Caccamo and Ms. Armstrong exchanged glances and smiled.

"We have a class for children with special needs," Mr. Caccamo began.

Auntie translated it into Chinese as "children who need something," and Mama and Father seemed confused. But when Jinna heard the words, she shuddered. She remembered what Priscilla had said about this class. All the difficult kids, all the ones with learning problems or physical disabilities or emotional problems or just plain bad behavior were lumped together in this Special Needs class.

The way Mr. Caccamo explained it, these students were separated out so they could get individual attention for their individual problems, but Priscilla had told her that their problems never got solved there. Unlike ESL class, where people graduated out of it as their English improved, Special Needs class was one of those places like the famous Taklimakan Desert in western China: those who go in never come out.

Ms. Linden seemed surprised and said she didn't think Special Needs class was the right solution for Jinna. "I think we should just leave Gina in ESL. I can teach her to speak English. I'm sure I can."

Mr. Caccamo disagreed. "She will keep attending ESL class. But she needs extra help. We need to do some further evaluation, Mr. and Mrs. Zhang, but I suspect Gina has a rare disorder called selective mutism. It's not a physical problem; it's what we call an anxiety disorder. Psychologists say that most children with this problem aren't deliberately choosing not to speak. They simply can't. They speak just fine at home, but not in school."

Even though Auntie couldn't translate all of these words, she got the message across. Jinna's problem had a name. This man understood it, and other children had the same problem.

"If Gina does have this disorder," Mr. Caccamo continued, "we need to start treating it before it goes on for too long."

He introduced Ms. O'Connell, the teacher with the wild red hair. She was the Special Needs teacher. She had a calm, friendly smile, Jinna thought.

Ms. O'Connell said she had never taught anyone with selective mutism before, but she had read up on it and would get some outside help. Mr. Caccamo explained that Jinna would spend time every afternoon in Special Needs, away from Ms. Armstrong's class. That alone felt like punishment to Jinna.

"So you can fix this problem?" Father asked, as if he still didn't believe it.

Mr. Caccamo told him they would try. He also recommended that her parents take Jinna to see a special kind of doctor, a psychiatrist, who could do a thorough evaluation and possibly recommend medication. But he couldn't *promise* he could fix the problem. Every child was different.

Father seemed relieved. He signed all the papers Mr. Caccamo gave him. He asked Mr. Caccamo to write down the words "selective mutism" and the name of a psychiatrist who spoke Chinese.

"They think they can help her!" he said to Mama on the way home. "Americans understand this problem. It even has a name. They have medication for it, and special programs right here at Jinna's school!"

Father seemed to be walking on air, but Jinna's feet felt like lead. The judgment was in. She was abnormal. Something was wrong with her. On Monday, she would have to go to the Special Needs class with all the weird kids. Everyone would think she was weird, too. She wouldn't be just silent. Her problem now had a label. All her teachers would work hard to cure her. No one would leave her alone.

CHAPTER twelve

... THIS WAS, the Princess finally realized, her last test. It would take more than cleverness and courage. This time she had to prove she was noble. What did it really mean to be noble? Being raised in a palace with the finest education? Having a fine character? Being high-minded? Being loved by all? She wasn't sure herself. How could she prove it if she couldn't even define it?

The market square was filled with hundreds and hundreds of strange faces, all the people of Far-Away, in the province of Over-the-Mountain. They were buzzing with anticipation. Pigsy stood next to her, holding his rake.

"I can do it, Pigsy," the Princess told her friend. "I've never felt better in my life."

"Of course you can," Pigsy answered. "After all, you are the real Princess. All you have to do is hold your head high no matter what happens. Then they will have no doubts about who you really are. This will be an easy test for you. Just be confident."

She smoothed and straightened her gown so that every embroidered dragon and phoenix shone with the brilliance of diamonds. She wore the jade pendant her mother had given her at birth. She had pulled her long black hair into a bun on the top of her head, the way ladies of the court wore their hair, with jade hairpins. She looked pure princess. But did she look noble?

"Ladies and gentlemen!" shouted Pigsy, standing on a platform made of three books. "May I present to you the Princess Jade-Blossom from the palace of the King in the City of Eternal Peace!"

The crowd grew silent. Most were unbelievers, but they were willing to give her a chance. The Princess held her skirts and stepped up to the platform like the lady she was.

She cleared her throat.

"Citizens of the Land of Far-Away, in the province Over-the-Mountain," she began. She spoke to them fluently, in their native tongue. The faces of the people below were blank. She tried to be as eloquent as possible. She knew how strong their doubts were.

"Fellow citizens of the Middle Kingdom and the world: I admire your land's lush green hills, your snow-capped mountains, your sparkling lakes and rivers teeming with fish, your fields rich with grain and fruit. Even your wild spaces are covered with juicy blackberries. Clearly, you live in a paradise."

The people clapped. It was a beautiful land, and people always like to hear flattery. Perhaps this would make them love her.

She continued. "I come to all of you today with humility, begging your forgiveness for dropping in so suddenly on the back of a crow." Yes, that sounded high-minded. The Princess threw back her shoulders. "It was not the way I would have chosen to arrive, or the timing I would have picked. Normally I would have come in a sedan chair, carried by the royal servants, accompanied by horses and elephants. I would have come to grace one of your festivals, at your invitation. That is what I would have preferred."

The crowd began murmuring with questions.

She wondered if Monkey King were listening. Was he disguised as one of the people below? Or as a dog? Or even as a tree? Of course he was listening.

"In my short life, I have never been asked to prove

I was a princess. Growing up in the palace, I called the king *Fuhuang,* Father King, and the queen *Muhou,* Mother Queen. Everyone addressed me as Princess Jade-Blossom. Which of *you* has had to prove you are really who your parents say you are?"

She heard more grumbling from the crowd. They still did not seem to believe she was a princess. What could she say that would convince them? She raised her chin.

"At the palace, I was educated in the fine arts. I learned to embroider two sides of the cloth at once, using tiny elegant stitches. I learned to sing and dance and play the *zheng,* the ancient zither. If you have such a zither here, I will play for you."

This time most of the grumbling seemed to come from the women. Perhaps they could also sing, dance, and embroider and wondered how these things could prove she was a princess. Her hands began to twist, but she kept her poise.

"I was taught to write with a brush and ink, and to memorize Tang dynasty poems and Yuan dynasty lyrics. I watched performances of Chinese opera."

Now everyone was mumbling again. Perhaps they thought princesses had easy lives and never had to study. They knew nothing of life in the palace! Her throat felt tight, but her words came out smoothly.

"I am fluent in every language and can understand problems of people in the farthest provinces. When I return to the palace, I will report to my father the kindness of the people of Far-Away, and he will reward you for your faithfulness."

"Are you blind?" shouted an old woman. "Can you not see *our* problem?"

The Princess stared out at the faces in front of her. Most of the people were dressed in simple clothing, but they did not look particularly poor. Nor did they appear to be suffering from any illness. How could she see their problems from looking at their faces?

"She has been among us for so long, and still she does not see what is wrong here!" a man shouted. "She is a fraud!"

What problem? What had she missed? Her vision blurred and she felt a strong desire to escape. Could the Crow come and get her now, to take her back to the palace? She looked up, but the Crow was nowhere in sight. Instead, the sun had disappeared behind a dark cloud.

The people's voices grew louder.

"A true princess would have noticed our problem!" one voice shouted.

"There is not a drop of compassion in her!"

"We need a real princess, not a fake one!" called out another.

"Seize her!"

"Imprison her!"

The crowd climbed onto the platform and surrounded her.

"No!" Jade-Blossom shouted. "You're mistaken! Tell me your problem and I will use my magic powers to fix it!" She could feel their heavy breath and sweating hands.

But she could not stop them. They seized her and dragged her off the platform. She walked as steadily as she could, keeping her shoulders back and her head high. The next thing she knew, she was inside a jail, a round, clear-walled tower where she had no privacy. They could watch her every move . . .

Jinna sat back on her heels and looked at the Princess, slumped under an upside-down glass on her bedside table. Her hair was starting to come out of the bun. The crowd of Yarn People was cheering, but Jinna felt sad. She had not meant for the story to turn out this way. She got mad at the crowd and swept them up and tossed them in the drawer. The Princess would not look at her.

Jinna crawled into bed and curled up, hugging her pillow. How could this have happened? How could the Princess have failed her test? The Princess shouldn't make mistakes. What did it mean to be a true princess? What problem had they expected her to solve? Would Monkey King come to save her? Jinna had no idea. For the time being, the Princess would have to stay in jail.

The heaviness inside her grew till Jinna thought she would sink through her bed, through the foundation of the house, through the fiery ball at the center of the earth, all the way to China.

On Saturday morning, when Mama came to wake her up, Jinna did not want to get out of bed.

"We all have to go to the restaurant now," Mama said. "Time to get moving." But Jinna shook her head and rolled over, closing her eyes again.

"I don't like to leave you alone. You'll feel better if you get up and come with us. Get dressed and I'll go make your breakfast."

But when Mama came back in ten minutes, Jinna had not moved.

"Do you feel OK?" Mama felt her forehead. Jinna shook her head. "OK, you can stay at home today. Call me if you need anything. I'll call you after the lunch hour rush."

Mama, Father, Auntie, and Uncle left, but Jinna stayed in bed. She didn't feel like reading or watching TV. She didn't even feel like playing with her Yarn People. Every time she looked at the Princess in her glass jail, she rolled over and faced the wall.

When Mama came home that evening, Jinna did

not speak to her. Jinna could no longer speak at all—even at home, even to Mama, even in Chinese. Jinna nodded or shook her head, but that was all she seemed to have the energy for.

On Sunday Jinna still couldn't speak, and no amount of pushing by her father would get her out of bed to go to the restaurant. Again, she spent most of the day lying in bed, trying to sleep.

Around four o'clock in the afternoon, she heard a tapping on her window and saw Priscilla's wide brown eyes. What was *she* doing here? Jinna shook her head and rolled over, but Priscilla let herself in the back door. Why hadn't Mama locked it? Jinna didn't know.

"Are you sick again? What's the matter?" Priscilla barged into her room and turned on the light.

Maybe if I ignore her, she'll go away, thought Jinna.

"What happened after school on Friday? I saw your parents and those teachers go into Mr. Caccamo's office. Was it bad? Are you in trouble? What did they say?"

Priscilla paused, as if she expected an answer. Jinna's eyes flooded up and she buried her head in her pillow. It was none of Priscilla's business. She should go away.

"Are they going to put you in Special Needs class? It's not really *that* bad. My brother says the teacher's really nice. It's just some of the fifth-grade boys are real jerks. I'll tell you which ones to watch out for."

But Jinna could tell from Priscilla's voice that she was worried.

Suddenly Priscilla noticed the Princess in her glass prison. "Omigosh, Gina. What happened to the Princess? Did I miss something? Why is she inside that glass? Is it good or bad?"

Jinna stared at the wall. She wished she were back in China.

Priscilla opened the drawer and found the little blue girl. Using Dorothy's voice, she said, "Princess, Princess, what have they done to you? Can I help?"

Jinna rolled over and looked at the Princess and Dorothy. She shook her head sadly.

"She's in jail, isn't she? Well, it's the third test. I'm sure she'll find her way out. She's brave and smart and—what was the other thing? Can Dorothy help her get out?"

Jinna shook her head and looked at the ceiling.

"Guess what!" Priscilla continued. "I found out that I don't say dumb things! My cousin told me. He said it's impossible. Stupid things, maybe, but not dumb things. You'll never guess why!"

Jinna didn't even try to guess.

"'Cause *dumb* doesn't really mean *stupid!* At least it didn't used to. In the olden days, *dumb* meant you couldn't talk. Ha! My cousin said no one would ever accuse me of being dumb! He says I talk too much. Do you think I talk too much?"

At the moment, yes, thought Jinna. But she said nothing. There it was—proof that Jinna was dumb. Just what she needed.

"Like 'deaf and dumb'—that's the way they used to describe people who couldn't hear or talk. I guess they just thought they were dumb because they never said anything, but I think that's ridiculous, don't you? I mean, look at you."

Jinna's short black hair was messed up from sleeping, and she had bags under her eyes.

"Well, usually you look a lot better than you do right now. But anyway, who can make up better stories than you? Have you been listening to those Young Authors' stories the kids have been reading aloud? They're so dumb! I mean they're so *stupid*. None of them is anywhere near as good as your Princess story. In fact, I haven't even been able to start writing my story this year. You know why?"

Jinna shook her head.

"'Cause I keep thinking about your story, about the Princess and the Monkey King and Pigsy and all their adventures. My stories seem so boring next to yours. But I had a good idea. Maybe it will help the teachers realize you don't belong in the Special

Needs class. You haven't started writing a Young Authors' story, have you?"

Jinna sat up and looked hard at Priscilla. What was she getting at?

"Well, maybe it's not such a good idea. Do you want to hear it?"

Jinna was skeptical, but she nodded.

"Well, I have a computer at home. Not a good one, but good enough to write on. It has a way of correcting your spelling. I was thinking I could—"

The fire in Jinna's eyes stopped her.

"Well, you probably don't want me to. I'll just tell you my idea and you can say no, OK? I was thinking I could type up your Princess story for you, and we could turn it in as a joint project—your story, but my typing."

Jinna started to sit up, rising like the fireball she had become the last time she was angry. Priscilla had promised to keep the Yarn People a secret! How could she even think of this?

"Or not!" Priscilla added quickly. "I mean, it's your story. It's not my story. Dorothy just watches. She never does anything. She wouldn't even have to be in the story. I should write my own story. But maybe I could just type up your story for you. When the teacher sees it, she'll know that you . . ."

Jinna didn't give Priscilla a chance to finish her

sentence. Jinna rose from the bed with anger all over her face, then fell back again, covering her head with her pillow. She felt miserable and vulnerable and betrayed. Priscilla went over to the bed and tried to pull the pillow off.

"OK, already, it was just a suggestion! I said you could say no! I was just trying to help. Just don't be mad at me, OK?" Priscilla pulled the pillow aside and looked into Jinna's eyes.

Silently, Jinna pleaded with Priscilla. *Don't tell my secret. Please don't do this to me,* she thought, wishing so much she could shout out her meaning. But suddenly, she didn't care anymore. She swept the Princess's glass prison onto the floor. It rolled across the carpet. Then she got back in bed and buried her face in the pillow. Why was Priscilla pressuring her like this? Everybody wanted her to do something she just couldn't do.

Priscilla picked up the glass and carefully placed the Princess back in it on Jinna's bedside table. "You'll figure out how to get her out of jail," she said. "I'm sure you will."

She left Jinna alone and let herself out the back.

C HAPTER **thirteen**

O N MONDAY, Jinna wanted to stay home
again. But Father dragged her out of bed,
and Mama started to dress her.

"School is your work. You have to go. No choice,"
Father said.

"I hope you can start that special class today,"
Mama said at breakfast, adding an egg to her rice
porridge. "It might be just what you need."

Jinna kept thinking of Priscilla's words: *Special
Needs class isn't that bad. The teacher's really nice.*

The sky was overcast but the day was warm as
Jinna walked to school. It was mid-April now, and
along the street she saw several cherry trees covered

with delicate pink blossoms. Many of the houses had gardens of tulips and daffodils. She looked more carefully than usual at the kids rushing in the door of the school, especially the fifth graders from other classes. Who was in the Special Needs class? They looked the same as everyone else. It wasn't the end of the world.

Jinna went to her regular class, and the other kids ignored her as usual. They had a spelling test, and even though she had studied, Jinna was sure she missed many of the words. Jinna had memorized the spellings easily, but she had a hard time recognizing the words when Ms. Armstrong read them aloud.

After lunch, Ms. Armstrong came to Jinna's desk and told her she would be going to Special Needs class with two other kids, Caitlin and Rickie. Caitlin looked normal but had trouble concentrating. Rickie's head and hands always shook.

Jinna's own hands started shaking, too. She hated new situations and new teachers. *Please don't make me go,* she wanted to beg Ms. Armstrong. But as usual, the words wouldn't come. So she followed Ms. Armstrong, Rickie, and Caitlin down the hall and into a classroom Jinna had never seen before.

"Gina, this is Mr. Brandon," Ms. Armstrong said, leading her to a tall young man with a brown ponytail. "He's the Special Needs teacher's aide. Why isn't

Ms. O'Connell here today?" she asked him.

"She called in sick and they couldn't find a substitute. She'll probably be back tomorrow," said Mr. Brandon. "Is this the new student I heard about?" He smiled at Jinna.

"Yes, this is Gina Zhang. Is it OK for her to start today, even though Ms. O'Connell isn't here?"

"It should be OK. I'm really not supposed to take new students when Ms. O'Connell isn't here, but Gina can just observe today, to get a sense of what we do," said Mr. Brandon.

Ms. Armstrong left Jinna there and went back to her class.

Jinna stood at the side of the classroom and looked around. The room, which had games and books as well as a white board for teaching, actually seemed friendly and welcoming. Rickie got out a game that looked like three-dimensional tic-tac-toe, and Caitlin and a friend began working on a puzzle. One girl with short, straight black hair like Jinna's sat in a wheelchair at the back of the room, alone. She was strapped in and couldn't seem to keep her head straight.

Suddenly, a storm of boys entered the room. There were only three of them, but they were big and loud enough for a gang. Jinna had noticed them picking on little kids on the playground. Their names were Jeremy, Jimmy, and Joe, but Priscilla always called them "Meanie, Miney, and Moe."

"Hey Mr. Brandon!" one of them said. "Gimme five!"

"Look who's here. A new girl," said another, leering at Jinna.

"It's the one who can't talk, isn't it?" said the biggest of the three. *He must be Meanie,* thought Jinna. "Don't worry, Mr. Brandon, we'll teach her!"

He came over to Jinna and stuck his face too close to hers. "My name is Joe. You say it—Joe." Then he grabbed her chin. "Joe! Say it! Joe!"

Jinna tried to pull back, but he held her chin too tightly. Her jaw clenched.

"Cut it, Joe. You guys sit down," Mr. Brandon said. "I've got something to show you."

"Why should we?" said another one.

But Joe let go of Jinna's chin and they followed Mr. Brandon to their seats. Jinna shrank to the back of the room and sat next to the girl in the wheelchair. The girl's name, Carrie, was embroidered on a sign that hung from the back of her chair. Carrie glanced at Jinna with a blank look, then cast her eyes down. Jinna wished she could talk to her.

"OK, guys," said Mr. Brandon, "we're going to start with math bingo."

"Let's not and say we did," said one of the boys.

"I hate that game!" said Joe.

But Mr. Brandon made them get out the math bingo cards and markers. All the students had to sit at a big table, with a card in front of them. Each card had different numbers printed on it, noticed Jinna, who had never played this game before.

Carrie had been left in a corner of the room. Without asking anyone, Jinna wheeled her over to the table and sat next to her, making sure Carrie got a card, too.

"I wouldn't bother. She can't play," said a boy.

Jinna looked at Mr. Brandon. "No. That's good. Let her play," he said.

Was that a smile on Carrie's face? Jinna wasn't sure. She had never met anyone like Carrie before but assumed she must have feelings and thoughts like anyone else.

"OK, guys, pay attention," said Mr. Brandon. "Jeremy! Joe! Eyes here. Quiet now. The first card is: B eight-times-two, plus three. That means it's in the B row. Can you figure out in your head what eight-times-two, plus three equals? Jimmy! Cut it out!"

Jimmy was covering his entire B row with markers. "Bingo!" he said.

"Stop it, Jimmy," said Mr. Brandon.

Jinna quickly calculated that the answer was nineteen. She didn't have a nineteen in her B row. She noticed that Carrie did. She pointed to the nineteen on Carrie's card, but Carrie just stared, so Jinna put a marker in Carrie's hand and guided it to the spot.

"OK, quiet now!" said Mr. Brandon. "The next one is harder. But you guys are fifth graders, so I'm sure you can do it. It's G sixty-divided-by-twelve."

"Forget it! We can't divide by twelve! That wasn't on the times table. What's the answer?" whined Jeremy.

Jinna found G five on her card and covered it. Carrie had G five, too, so Jinna helped her cover it.

The game went on. Every other sentence out of Mr. Brandon's mouth seemed to be "Quiet" or "Settle down now" or "Pay attention." Meanie, Miney, and Moe shouted out of turn, laughed, messed up their bingo cards, and made it hard for everyone else to hear Mr. Brandon or get his attention. Most of the other kids seemed amused by them, but Jinna was not.

What a waste of time, she thought. *Ms. Armstrong has been teaching us how to add fractions, which I learned in fourth grade. And now I have to spend my afternoon on simple division and multiplication.*

But at least no one was demanding that she speak. That was a relief.

The kids were having trouble concentrating, so Mr. Brandon decided to give them a fifteen-minute recess on the playground. When he announced it, Meanie, Miney, and Moe whooped with delight.

Jinna, too, was relieved to get outside on a rare sunny day. She wheeled Carrie out to the playground and stood next to her near a wall, watching the other kids kick balls and play on the bars.

Someone had carefully painted Carrie's fingernails with sparkly silver polish, and she wore tiny blue star-shaped earrings. Her wheelchair was purple and had cat stickers neatly arranged across the back. Jinna wondered what was wrong with her, that she was in a wheelchair and didn't talk.

What are you thinking? Jinna mentally asked her, as if thoughts could fly across silent space. *Do you like being outside in the sunshine? I do.*

Mr. Brandon stood near the door, watching the kids. Suddenly, Jinna heard a scream. Rickie had fallen off the bars and hit his head. Mr. Brandon and the kids rushed over to him.

"He's bleeding!" shouted one girl.

"Rickie! Are you OK?" Mr. Brandon knelt next to the boy. Rickie got up but seemed very unsteady, and Mr. Brandon began walking him back into the building. "I'll be back in just a minute," he shouted at the kids. "He needs to see the nurse." A cloud passed over the sun, and Jinna felt cold.

As soon as Mr. Brandon went inside, Meanie,

Miney, and Moe appeared in front of Jinna and Carrie. "He's outta here!" one said. "Now we get to try out the wheelchair!"

Before Jinna realized what was happening, Joe had unbuckled Carrie, lifted her from her wheelchair, and sat her on the ground, propping her up against the wall. Carrie immediately slumped over. Jinna was shocked.

"Don't worry," he said to Jinna. "She don't mind."

She looked at Carrie, who had a stunned and frightened look in her eyes.

Jimmy jumped into the wheelchair and Jeremy fought with him. "Forget it, Jimmy! It was my idea. I get to go first!" But Joe had already begun pushing Jimmy around the playground. Joe got it going as fast as possible, then let go. Jimmy raised his arms and whooped as he sped across the playground.

"Yee-haw!" he shouted, just before crashing into the fence.

Jinna wanted to yell at the boys, to tell them what jerks they were, grab the wheelchair back, run and tell Mr. Brandon, tell Mr. Caccamo, tell someone— anyone, to get them to stop. But she couldn't. Her throat was so tight she could barely breathe.

The other kids just stared at the boys, afraid to intervene. Jinna ran to the door and looked inside. If she could find Mr. Brandon, she could pull his hand till he came out and saw the problem. But she didn't see any teachers at all. And she didn't want to run inside and leave Carrie alone.

Jinna returned to Carrie's side and tried to prop her up into a near-sitting position. The sunshine was rapidly disappearing as the sky turned gray. She took Carrie's hand and felt a small squeeze back. Carrie seemed scared and confused. Carrie was a prisoner inside her own body, Jinna thought, just like the Princess inside her glass jail.

A surge of anger ran through Jinna. She stood up and ran after the boys. They were moving so fast they nearly knocked her down as they flew past her.

"Out of the way, stupid!" shouted Jeremy, who was pushing now. The chair crashed into the fence again, tossing Joe onto the blacktop with a yelp. Jinna caught up to them and grabbed the arms of the chair.

"Forget it! You don't get a turn!" said Joe.

Jinna pointed to Carrie, making her face as stern and angry as she could.

"Sorry. You'll have to speak up. I can't catch your meaning," said Joe in a mocking voice. "Offa that chair." He tried to shove her hands away, but she held on tightly.

"Stupid girl! Go away!" Jimmy ran over, making it three large boys against one tiny girl. They forced her hands off the chair and jerked it away. Jinna noticed several dents in Carrie's beautiful purple chair. Two of the boys took the chair and sped across the playground with it. Joe stayed and towered over Jinna.

Where is Mr. Brandon? thought Jinna. *He said he'd be back in a minute!*

"You are dumber than I thought," Joe said, shoving his chest in her face to make her feel short. "I can see why they put you in Special Needs. But don't worry. I'll teach you to talk." He took her arm and twisted it behind her back, pushing it higher so it hurt. "Say 'uncle,'" he said, laughing.

The pain shot through her arm and she grimaced. She had seen other kids do this, but no one had ever done it to her. He twisted her arm harder and jerked her wrist higher behind her back.

A garbled squeal shot out of her mouth.

"Good start. Now let's hear it—'uncle.'" He jerked her arm again.

Another yelp escaped from her.

"You're making progress. Now say it." Jinna could not stand the pain. No one had ever deliberately hurt her before, and she couldn't believe it was happening.

"Just say 'uncle' and I'll let you go. UNCLE." Another jerk. She felt like she was going to faint.

Suddenly Mr. Brandon appeared at her side.

"Joe!" he shouted, grabbing Joe's hand and making

him let go. "What do you think you're doing?"

Mr. Brandon grabbed the wheelchair and rushed back to Carrie. He lifted her gently into the chair and checked to see if she was OK.

"We're in trouble now," said Jimmy.

"Bright idea, Joe," said Jeremy.

"Outta my face, dumbheads," said Joe. He started to strut away, but then turned back to Jinna. Her arm hung limp and injured at her side. "You better keep your mouth shut," he warned her.

"Like she's gonna tell." Jeremy let out a loud cackle. "That's a good one."

Joe shot him a withering look and then trotted across the playground as if nothing had happened. But Mr. Brandon went straight after him. Meanie, Miney, and Moe weren't going to get away this time.

"Everybody back to class!" shouted Mr. Brandon. He grabbed Joe by the elbow and dragged him away.

Jinna held her arm as if it had been broken. An adult had come out to wheel Carrie back inside, and the other kids were heading back to class. No one asked Jinna how she was.

A light rain wet her hair and cheeks.

CHAPTER fourteen

MR. CACCAMO came into the Special Needs classroom and took the three boys away. Carrie spent the rest of the afternoon in the nurse's office. The other students sat quietly, working on a paper that Mr. Brandon had given them. Jinna had a feeling that he might be in even bigger trouble than Meanie, Miney, and Moe.

Jinna's left arm felt so bruised and twisted that she couldn't concentrate on the worksheet. She watched the hands of the clock until three o'clock, when she could go home.

When the bell finally rang, Jinna went back to Ms. Armstrong's class to get her backpack and coat.

Priscilla noticed Jinna's limp arm the minute she entered the room. "Omigosh, Gina, what happened to you?"

Jinna was fighting back tears as she gathered her books and homework and struggled to stuff them into her backpack without using her left hand.

"Here, I'll help," Priscilla said, holding the backpack open. Then she helped Jinna put on her jacket. "Is it broken?" Priscilla whispered. "You should see a doctor."

Jinna shook her head vigorously, biting her lip to hold back the tears. In a minute she was out of the classroom, down the hall, and out the front door of the school. Priscilla followed close behind. The rain was heavier now. Joe was nowhere to be seen in the crowd of kids, but Jinna rushed anyway.

Across the main street and half a block away, near the yellow house on the corner, the tears began to flow down Jinna's cheeks.

Priscilla and Jinna were both soaking wet by the time they reached Jinna's house. Priscilla followed her inside. Jinna went straight to the living room and curled up on the couch. Priscilla found a shawl and tucked it around her. Then she sat at the other end of the couch in the dark living room.

"It was one of those jerks, wasn't it?" Priscilla said. "Meanie, Miney, and Moe—right?"

Jinna barely nodded her head. Sobs were shaking her body now, and she cradled her arm on her lap as if it were an injured child.

"I hate them. They pick on everybody. One time one of them picked up my little brother on the playground and held him upside down by one foot. Do you believe it? He was only in kindergarten then. The guy nearly dropped my brother on the cement. What did they do to you? Let me see."

She helped Jinna out of her jacket and sweater. Jinna rolled up the sleeve of her turtleneck shirt, and Priscilla looked at the arm. Jinna rubbed her shoulder and winced. Then she buried her face in a pillow and sobbed harder.

"Should I call 9-1-1?" Priscilla asked. Jinna shook her head, still sobbing too hard to think. "Seriously, Gina, if it's broken or something, you should see a doctor. Did you hear the bone crack?"

Priscilla's way of comforting, of course, was to talk nonstop. She began relating stories about all the terrible things she had heard about Jeremy, Jimmy, and Joe. She had seen them twist kids' arms up behind their backs. "Is that what happened?" Priscilla asked, demonstrating it on herself. Jinna nodded.

"Ohhhh," said Priscilla. "Do you want me to call your mother?"

Jinna wasn't sure.

"I probably should," she continued. "What's the number?" Priscilla stood up, walked into the kitchen, found the cordless phone, and brought it into the living room. She held the phone out to Jinna.

"Just dial the number, and I'll do the talking. Come on, Gina. You don't have to talk. I'll talk to your mom, or your aunt, or whoever. Someone will understand English, won't they?"

Jinna sighed and nodded. Priscilla held the phone while Jinna punched in the numbers with her right hand.

"Can I speak to Gina's mother, please? . . . Gina's mama. Right." Priscilla waited for Jinna's mom to pick up. "Hi. I'm Gina's friend. Gina is at home. She needs you. She is hurt. Please come home now." For once, Priscilla spoke in short sentences, easy to understand. But Jinna's mother still had to hand the phone over to Auntie to translate. Finally, Priscilla got the message across.

Jinna still felt uncertain.

"It'll be OK," said Priscilla. "She's coming home. I gotta go now. My mom's working and my little brother doesn't go to after-school day care anymore, so I have to baby-sit. You stay right here. Want anything?" Jinna shook her head, but Priscilla went to the refrigerator, got out a bottle of Yakult, opened it, and gave it to Jinna. Jinna half-smiled. Priscilla waved and smiled her gap-toothed smile as she left.

As soon as Priscilla was gone, Jinna closed her eyes and escaped. But instead of a grassy field of wild-flowers, with little girls chasing butterflies and flying kites, all she could imagine was the inside of the Princess's jail. The Princess was surrounded by bright lights and people looking in. A cold, dark dungeon with rats and cockroaches would have been better than the glass prison.

Jinna was in jail with her, looking out at the faces: dark and light skin, curly brown hair and straight black hair, freckles and wrinkles, bushy eyebrows and pink cheeks, pretty black curls and kinky braids, wavy blond hair and short stubby black hair. The eyes were brown and blue and green, slanted and round, with short eyelashes and long curly ones. They were all staring at her, mocking and judging. They thought she was dumb and abnormal.

A deep sadness overwhelmed Jinna, and she began shaking. She opened her eyes and looked around the living room, familiar yet strange today. She stood up slowly and walked as if underwater to her room, still cradling her sore left arm. The Princess was in her glass jail on the bedside table. With her right hand, Jinna opened the drawer that held all the other Yarn People. She hated them.

She picked up a handful, took them into the

bathroom, and threw them into the toilet. Then she ran back for another handful, until all the Yarn People, even Monkey King and Pigsy, were soaking sadly in the water. She closed the lid and wept.

Not long afterward, Mama found her there. "Did you throw up?" she asked. "What's wrong?"

Jinna fell into Mama's arms like a rag doll.

CHAPTER **fifteen**

MAMA AND AUNTIE called a taxi and rushed Jinna to the doctor, Auntie's doctor in Chinatown. While Dr. Tsai examined her, Jinna remained silent. Mama explained to the doctor that Jinna had not been speaking in class and that the school counselor had recommended some kind of medicine.

Dr. Tsai took an X-ray and announced that her arm was not broken. He examined her throat and asked questions that she could answer with a nod or a head-shake. Finally he gave her a prescription for a medicine that was supposed to help her relax.

Mama and Auntie felt relieved after the doctor's

visit, but Jinna did not. Her biggest problem was not in her body, she knew. It was at school. But she could not bring herself to explain this, not even to her mother. The metal band had closed around her throat so tightly now that no words came out anymore, no matter where she was.

By the time Jinna got home from the doctor, her arm hurt a little less. But she went straight to bed. Mama soothed her and kissed her forehead as if she had a fever. But Jinna felt cold and stiff inside.

The next day, Jinna didn't go to school. Mama went to work, and Jinna spent the day feeling miserable. She lay on the sofa, thinking what a failure she had been at school in America. Whatever happened to becoming the New Jinna? That was a joke.

As the clock hands neared three o'clock, though, she began to look out the front window for Priscilla. At last she saw the large purple coat round the corner. Jinna opened the door and let Priscilla in.

Priscilla was breathing hard from running. She sat down at the kitchen table. "Gina, I found out what happened on the playground yesterday. Everybody is talking about it at school." Her eyes were shining.

Jinna sat down, too, confused.

"Mr. Brandon told Ms. Armstrong what you did to get Carrie's wheelchair back, and she told our class," Priscilla continued. "You stood up for Carrie when nobody else would! And you went after the meanest, toughest boy in the school. That was so brave of you!"

Jinna shook her head. She wasn't brave! She was stupid. She had gone up against the school bully, and he had hurt her badly.

"Carrie's mom wants to meet you and thank you in person," Priscilla continued. "You won't believe how Ms. Armstrong described you! She said you were—wait, I forget! Oh yeah—'good-hearted.' Do you believe it? Isn't that cool?"

Jinna looked at Priscilla's eyes to see if she was joking. *Good-hearted?* Jinna had not heard this word before, but she could guess what it meant. It sounded like a good translation for the Chinese word *ren*. *Ren* meant noticing when people needed help and helping them, not for selfish reasons or out of pity but because it was right. It was one of the easiest characters to write, but very hard to translate into English. *Good-hearted,* thought Jinna. *That's it.* But what a surprise to hear someone describing her that way!

Priscilla shook her head in amazement. "Lots of people came up to me today and told me how cool they thought it was that you stood up for Carrie," she said. "I had to come and tell you."

Jinna was not used to such praise, and she felt embarrassed and confused. Who would want to be like Jinna, silent and scared, silly and strange? It was too much to have Priscilla looking at her with those admiring eyes. Jinna stood up and fidgeted with the edge of her sweatshirt.

"What's going on with the Princess today?" asked Priscilla. "Can I see?"

Jinna tried to block the way to her bedroom, but Priscilla paid no attention and plowed right past her. When she got to the doorway, Priscilla froze.

On Jinna's bedside table, the Princess remained slumped in her glass jail. All the other Yarn People were spread out neatly on the floor. Mama had rescued them and laid them out to dry, but now they looked skinny and pathetic.

"Omigosh, Gina, what happened to them?" Priscilla rushed in and picked up a few of the limp Yarn People. "You've got to tell me!"

But Jinna's mouth stayed tightly shut. How could she tell Priscilla what she had done?

Priscilla found Dorothy. She held Dorothy against her chest and tried to smooth out her dress. She found Pigsy and Monkey King and the Silver-Horned Monster. They all looked terrible.

"Why did you wreck them up?" asked Priscilla. "Just 'cause that stupid bully hurt you? You can't take it out on the Yarn People. The Princess wouldn't do that, and you know it."

I'm not like the Princess, thought Jinna. *Not at all.* She focused on the drawer handles of her dresser and tried to think of something else. But Priscilla's words echoed in her mind: "That was so brave of you!" *Am I brave?* Jinna wondered. *Then why do I always feel so scared and dumb and alone?*

"Anyway, look what I did last night." Priscilla opened her backpack and took out a stack of pages. She tried to hand it to Jinna, but Jinna backed away.

"No, I'm serious, Gina. You have to read it. Come here," Priscilla commanded her.

She sat on Jinna's bed. Jinna reluctantly sat next to her and took the papers. The title page said:

Adventures of a Princess
By Gina Zhang

She looked up at Priscilla in confusion.

"Please don't be mad at me," Priscilla began. "It's your story. I typed it up on my computer for you. It took forever. It's not right, I know. There are parts we have to fix. Just let me know, and I'll fix them."

Jinna looked at the next page. It read:

Once upon a time, a Princess named ??? lived in a palace with her father the king and mother the queen in the city of ???

One day a big black crow flew to the palace and he picked up the Princess ???. She was very scared. She thought she would fall. They flew and flew over fields and rivers and ????

"No!" she shouted. "Put me down!" But the Crow kept flying.

Jinna dropped the story down on her quilt. *Why did you do this?* she thought. *This story is about my own personal world. Why would you want to reveal it to other people? Everyone will laugh at me, just as they laughed at the Raindrop story. They will tease me and call me "Princess."*

"It's for Young Authors' Day," explained Priscilla, excited. "Don't you get it? When Ms. Armstrong reads it, she'll know you're not dumb. She'll know you can make up great stories, and that you understand a lot of English. I don't have to tell her I helped. If you hand in a really great story for Young Authors' Day, maybe everyone will see that you're OK and you won't have to go to that Special Needs class. Do you think it will work?"

What a good friend, thought Jinna. *But still . . .*

"You don't have to hand it in if you don't want to," continued Priscilla. "In fact, it's not even finished. I put question marks where I forgot things, and I don't know how it ends. The rough draft is due on Thursday. If you want me to help you correct it and add the ending . . ."

Her voice faltered as Jinna's face hardened. *Priscilla promised not to tell anyone about the Yarn People. Now she is breaking her promise.*

"I won't tell anyone about the Yarn People—how you act out the story with them," said Priscilla, as if reading her mind. "Nobody has to know about that. Just write the story down."

Jinna was torn. It wasn't a bad idea. It might work. Anything was worth trying, if it would get her out of the class with those horrible boys. But she had always kept her stories secret. As long as she did, no one could make fun of them. How could American kids understand about Monkey King and Pigsy?

"I can help you finish it," continued Priscilla, reaching for the story. "But I need to know the names . . ."

Jinna grabbed the story back from her and held it behind her. Then she stuffed it under her pillow and sat on it. No. Impossible. She couldn't risk it. She couldn't let the kids and teachers know who she really was. If they did, they would never like her.

"Come on, Gina, don't be mad," said Priscilla. "It's a great idea. Think about it. I mean, imagine Ms. Armstrong reading it to the whole class, and everybody clapping."

The image of all those faces staring at her horrified Jinna. What if they didn't clap but laughed instead? Priscilla tried to get the story out from under Jinna's pillow, but Jinna blocked the way.

Finally, Priscilla stood back. "OK. I don't need it back. I have it on my computer anyway. If you change your mind and decide you want to hand it in, you can read it over tonight and mark anything you want me to change. Then I'll type in all the corrections tomorrow."

Jinna shook her head firmly.

"Or not," said Priscilla. "You decide. I didn't do it for fun, you know. I did it for you."

Jinna pointed to the door.

"OK, but anyway, I still want to know how it ends. How does the Princess get out of jail? What happens to her? She probably goes back to the palace, right? But how does she get there? Does Monkey King use his magic? Does she get back her magic powers? Then how . . ."

Weariness settled over Jinna. She fell back onto her pillow and rolled toward the wall. She didn't know how the story ended. How could she know?

Priscilla took the hint. "Well, if you change your mind, let me know," she said as she left.

In the silence, Jinna couldn't help thinking about Priscilla's questions. How *would* the Princess get out of jail? What *would* be the best ending for her? Would she just go back to the palace and take up her old life?

Jinna tried to put the story out of her mind, but Priscilla had flipped a switch in Jinna's head. Like that other princess who could feel the pea under her mattress, the one Ms. Armstrong had once talked about in class, Jinna could feel that bundle of pages under her pillow. She tried to pretend it was not there. But it *was* there. And she couldn't help wondering what her story looked like, all typed up in English. Jinna reached under the pillow and pulled out the pages. She sat up and began reading.

Printed on paper, in Priscilla's words, the story didn't have quite the same magic. It was just a story. It was an interesting one, though. The part about crossing the bathtub and rescuing Dorothy actually sounded a lot better the way Priscilla had written it. Big cliffs, not shampoo bottles, blocked the way, and the waterfall was loud and frightening. The Princess sounded so brave. She was brave.

Then what was she doing in that stupid jail? And how would she get out? Jinna could not think of a good ending.

Instead, she took a pencil out of her backpack. She crossed out the ??? parts and wrote in "Jade Blosm" and "City of Long Pese" and "montans" in carefully formed English letters. Her spelling might be wrong, she figured, but Priscilla would fix it on her computer. She added in words and sentences and descriptions and conversations. The more she wrote, the more she liked the story. It really *was* her story. Priscilla had gotten it right, mostly. But it was missing a lot of the detail that only Jinna could add.

If she worked hard enough, maybe she could even put the magic back in.

Chapter sixteen

AT EIGHT O'CLOCK, Jinna heard a key in the door. *It must be Mama*, she thought, *coming home after the dinner rush to check on me.* Jinna shoved the story under her pillow and pretended she had been reading a book. But the footsteps coming down the hall were heavier than Mama's.

To Jinna's surprise, Father stood at the door to her room. He held his left hand in his right. Jinna could see a big white bandage wrapped around his index finger. He looked sort of stunned.

"What happened?" she asked. "Are you hurt?" She jumped up and went to him.

"I cut myself, but I'm OK."

"How did it happen? Is it badly cut?" Jinna asked, following him into the kitchen. He sat down at the kitchen table, and she put some water on the stove to boil for tea.

"I was chopping pork," he said. "It's a deep cut. It bled so much I thought I had lost my finger, but it ended up only needing three stitches. Dr. Tsai sewed it up for me."

"That sounds awful. Does it hurt?" Jinna asked as she sprinkled a few dried tea leaves in Father's mug and set it near the stove.

"Only a little now. Uncle insisted I go home," said Father. "What were you doing? Your homework?"

"Yeah. My friend brought it over."

"Good," he said. "Have you spoken in class yet?"

"No." Here it came. The lecture. Jinna didn't want to look at him, but when she met his gaze, his eyes were soft. He seemed almost sad.

He held up his bandaged finger, then stretched out his other hand. "This isn't the first time I hurt my hand. Did I ever tell you that story?"

Jinna shook her head.

"When I was six years old," he said, "I was very small and timid. I didn't want to go to school, but my parents insisted. One day at school, when I was only in first grade, my book fell on the floor. When I went to pick it up, I accidentally stepped on the book. By bad luck, a picture of Chairman Mao, head of all China, was on that page. In those days, Chinese people almost worshipped Mao. To show such disrespect was not just a mistake but a crime."

The water was boiling. Jinna got up and poured hot water in Father's mug, set the cover on it, and placed it in front of him.

"I knew immediately I had done something very wrong," Father continued. "I hoped no one would notice. But my teacher noticed, and so did my classmates. My teacher took me to the principal's office. I was so scared. The principal wasn't there, but a group of radical teenage bullies was in his office. They screamed at me and tried to make me admit I hated Chairman Mao. That wasn't true! But I didn't know what to say. Then they said they would punish me. One big teenager stomped on my foot. Another took my right hand, the one that had dropped the book, and bent my fingers back till they broke. I screamed and screamed."

Jinna sat frozen, frightened out of her mind. Could such a terrible thing actually have happened to *her father*?

Father showed her his right hand. Three of his fingers were bent slightly to the right. She had noticed this before but never thought to ask why.

"You didn't see a doctor?" she asked.

He laughed. "The Cultural Revolution was going on in China. Everyone was attacking the doctors, too. They didn't have time to fix fingers on little boys in country villages. But after that, I didn't speak."

Jinna thought she had not heard correctly. "You didn't speak? What do you mean?"

"For ten years, I didn't speak. Not at home, not at school. I couldn't say a word."

Jinna stared at him. Why hadn't he ever told her this before?

Father looked at his broken fingers, then at his broken daughter. "When I saw you develop the same problem, I didn't want to believe it. I didn't want you to go through what I did. I wanted you to be normal, get good grades, not be afraid of anything."

Jinna could scarcely believe what he was saying.

Her father continued. "I thought things would be different for you. Life is better in America. The schools are not as hard. The government doesn't go crazy and make people hurt each other. People can get rich here."

Jinna stared at his misshapen fingers, still shocked. Was this the same father who had ordered her to speak at school?

"Nothing bad has ever happened in your life," he said. "You should be happy." He blew across his tea to make the leaves sink and took a sip.

The teasing voices of her classmates in China flashed across Jinna's mind, then the taunts of Joe and the pain as he twisted her arm. "They think I'm stupid at school," she said bitterly. "They think I can't do the work."

"Can you?"

"Yes." Jinna looked hard in his eyes. "Do you think I have this problem because you had it?"

Father shifted in his seat. "I talked on the phone to that doctor yesterday, the one that your counselor recommended. He told me that many children who stop speaking have a mother or father who had the same problem as a child."

"So I inherited it? From you?" Jinna shook her head in disbelief. All this time Father had been holding her responsible for her ailment, and now she was learning that it was not in her throat but in her genes. Could this be true?

Father examined the tea leaves in his cup. Then he looked at her and added, "I didn't know that before. I thought I should tell you."

A wave of relief washed over her. It wasn't entirely her fault. "But *Baba*," she asked tentatively, using the Chinese word for *Dad*, "you have no trouble speaking now. How did you start speaking again?"

He smiled. "By the time I reached sixteen, it got easier. I don't know why."

"Do you think I'll outgrow it, too? Will I have to wait ten years?" she asked.

"I think it will be easier for you. In America, they understand about this problem and can treat it."

Thoughts rushed through Jinna's head. "When you were little," she began hesitantly, "did the teachers try to make you speak?"

"Oh, yes, all the time. The kids teased me—first the boys, and later the girls. The teachers called on me and lowered my grades when I didn't answer."

"But you learned."

"Yes, of course I learned. You can learn without speaking."

"You can learn without speaking." Jinna repeated her father's sentence. That's what she had wanted to believe all along, but nobody seemed to think it was possible. Now here was her father, who knew more about this than all the teachers, confirming it.

Jinna looked up at Father, who was again examining his two hands. "I can learn without speaking," she said again.

Father looked her in the eye. "Of course you can. It's just more difficult that way."

A weight lifted from Jinna's heart. She wanted to run to Father and hug him, but that wasn't the way people acted in her family. How could she let him know how glad she was that he had told her? It must have been hard for him to show her his weak side. She wanted to show her gratitude and respect for him. "I'll add some more hot water to your tea," she offered. "Do you want a rice cake, too?"

He smiled and nodded. "I just want you to be normal and happy," he said. "Not suffering like I was."

That night, in Jinna's room, the Princess escaped from her glass prison with the help of Pigsy, Dorothy, and Monkey King. Monkey King said a magic spell over Pigsy, who turned into a handsome young farmer. The Princess fell in love with him and moved to his farmhouse, where they raised hundreds and hundreds of pigs but never killed one for meat.

It wasn't a great ending, but it was an ending. Jinna wrote it all down as neatly as she could, so Priscilla could type it up on the computer. On separate sheets of paper, she drew illustrations of each scene with colored pencils her mother had bought for her. She didn't go to bed until after three in the morning.

Jinna would have a story for Young Authors' Day, like all the American kids. She would truly be the New Jinna now.

Better yet, she would be Gina. But not the dumb Gina they thought she was at school. She would decide who this American Gina would be.

CHAPTER **seventeen**

THE NEXT DAY at school, Gina handed her story back to Priscilla. Priscilla glanced at the new ending, grinned, and slipped the story into her backpack.

In Special Needs class that afternoon, Gina was relieved to see that Ms. O'Connell was back. Gina noticed that her hair looked like frayed orange yarn.

In front of everyone in the class, Ms. O'Connell praised Gina for helping Carrie get back her wheelchair. Later, quietly, she asked Gina if she had a tape recorder and would be willing to tape herself speaking English at home. Gina wasn't sure she could do this, but she nodded anyway. Then Ms. O'Connell suggested they set a goal: one English word, whispered in her ear, by May first. It could be any word. Gina smiled and nodded. *How about "Guess what!"* she thought.

Meanie, Miney, and Moe mostly ignored Gina in class and on the playground. With Ms. O'Connell and Mr. Brandon watching every minute, they had no choice.

Carrie appeared to be fine. Gina wheeled her around in the early April sunshine, and Carrie seemed to enjoy the sun on her arms. Once Joe shot a menacing glance toward Gina, but he had no power to hurt her today. Besides, Pigsy was in her pocket.

After school, Priscilla invited Gina over to her house to finish the story. This time Gina agreed. Father had returned to work today, so no one would be at home for hours. Who would know that Gina wasn't there?

Gina watched Priscilla slowly type in the changes. Priscilla showed her how to check for spelling mistakes. Gina wished she had a software program like that in her head, especially during spelling tests.

When she had finished, Priscilla printed the whole thing out. It was ten pages long now, and it looked very impressive. Gina held it in her hand like a delicate jade vase. She couldn't believe it was her story, and yet she knew it was. Of all the Monkey King books she had read, none had a story anything like her Princess story. And despite all the help that Priscilla had given her, this was Gina's story, from beginning to end.

"Done!" Gina said, with a smile.

"Not exactly," said Priscilla. "This is just a rough draft. We have to hand this in tomorrow for Ms. Armstrong to correct. Then we're supposed to make the changes she suggests and print out a final copy. After that comes the fun part," she said, smiling slyly. She loped across the room and grabbed her backpack. From inside, she pulled out a brand-new book with a hard white cover and clean white pages. "See? It's a blank book! We each get one. Here, I'll show you."

Priscilla took the first page of Gina's story and cut out a big chunk of text, giving it rounded edges. Gina gasped, seeing the scissors chop into her work.

"Don't worry. I'll print you out another copy. What you do is you cut your story into sections and paste them onto the pages, like this." Priscilla held the cut-out section at the bottom of a page. "See, you have to leave room for a picture above the words. The first page will be the title page, so the story begins on the second page."

Gina took the book in her hands and marveled at

how white and real it looked. She ran her fingers over the smooth cover. "Here?" Gina asked, pointing to the front cover.

"That's where you write the title and your name. You can also draw a picture there."

"A picture of Princess."

"Yes. All dressed in pink. That would look great."

Gina felt happier than she had felt in a long time, ever since leaving China. She would have a book with a story she had made up and pictures she drew herself. She hugged the book and smiled her biggest smile at Priscilla.

"Sank you, Pasilla. I sank you very mush." Her voice was soft but firm.

Priscilla sat back with a huge grin on her face. "Do you really like it? You were so mad at first. I was afraid you would hate it."

Gina's face fell. She had forgotten about keeping the Princess a secret. Now Ms. Armstrong and the whole class would know about her imaginary world. Was she ready for this? She still wasn't sure.

"Everyone will think your story is very cool," Priscilla said. But to Gina's surprise, Priscilla stood up and looked away, as if hiding her face.

"Whassa matta?" Gina asked.

"I haven't even started writing my story yet. Every time I come up with an idea, I hate it and throw it away. Ms. Armstrong will kill me if I don't turn something in tomorrow."

Gina was shocked. Priscilla had spent hours on Gina's story and hadn't even started her own yet. Why hadn't she realized this?

"I help?" she asked. But Gina could not help, and Priscilla knew it.

"No. You go home. I'll work on it after dinner. Mine won't be very good anyway," said Priscilla.

Gina took her rough draft and the blank book and walked home slowly, trying to think of a way she could help Priscilla, her best friend, who wanted the whole world to know Gina was smart, even though it meant she might lose Gina to the other girls. Priscilla was like a precious gem, and Gina had been treating her like an everyday stone.

Gina got ready for bed on time that night but did not feel sleepy. She collected all her Yarn People and had a long talk with them, especially the Princess. It was Jade-Blossom's story, after all. How would she feel about a bunch of American kids and teachers knowing all about her? To Gina's surprise, Princess Jade-Blossom liked the idea. She wanted the world to know how brave and clever she was, and she was delighted that the cover picture would make her look so beautiful.

Pigsy was pleased, too. He thought he came out sounding very loyal and true. It was hard to tell how Monkey King felt. One minute he liked the story, the next minute he mocked it. Dorothy fretted the most. She thought she looked too plain in the pictures, and she wanted a bigger speaking role. Gina redrew Dorothy to make her look more attractive and tried to think of more words for her to say.

Then Gina stopped drawing and looked at all the Yarn People. "But if they know about you, what will I have left that's all my own?" she asked.

Monkey King laughed. "All your own? Do you think this one story is the only one you have in your head? There are thousands more stories where this one came from."

Gina paused. It was true, of course. Why hadn't she thought of that before? She could let her teacher and classmates see this one story, just so they would know she had a brain behind her silent exterior. But then she would still be free to make up new stories, with new characters. As long as she had an imagination, she would always have a private world no one else knew about.

"Yes!" shouted Pigsy. "We'll all go to school, and they will see how cool we are!"

In that case, the story had to be perfect. Yet something about it wasn't quite right. The more Gina thought about it, the more she knew what the problem was. It was the ending. The Princess had not yet passed her final test. She needed another chance to prove to the people of Far-Away that she was truly noble and that she cared about finding out what their problem was.

Yes, that was it. Being noble meant more than making a beautiful speech. It was showing that you care, the way Priscilla cared about Gina. Everyone had described Gina as good-hearted, but Priscilla was the most good-hearted of all.

Suddenly an idea began to form in Gina's head. She found some beige yarn and pink and blue felt and began making some Yarn People that had been missing all along. Without them, the Land of Far-Away had no future. *That* was their problem, obviously! But how would the Princess solve it? What would the exact test be?

Gina thought and worked till after midnight but still couldn't come up with the right ending.

In the morning, the Princess, Pigsy, and Monkey King insisted on going to school in Gina's pocket. The Princess wanted to see Sheliya and Michelle and Kylie and Henry and Carrie one more time before she became famous at Hilltop Elementary. Pigsy wanted to see the teacher with the fire-red hair.

Monkey King even wanted to challenge Big Bad Joe to a duel, but Gina talked him out of it.

Gina took one last look at her rough draft before putting it in her backpack. Even though the ending wasn't right yet, the story sounded good—much better than she had ever expected. How could she ever thank Priscilla enough? She hummed all the way to school.

Ms. Armstrong acted as though the rough drafts of the Young Authors' story were just an ordinary homework assignment. "Put them in this box on my desk, and let's get to work on the daily geography questions," she said. Gina felt far from ordinary as she put her draft in the teacher's box.

Priscilla came rushing in late and slapped a few thin pieces of paper onto the pile of stories. She flashed a weak smile at Gina and shook her head. Gina felt terrible.

As soon as the recess bell rang, everyone ran off for the playground. Gina and Priscilla found Carrie and pushed her around in her wheelchair. Gina wondered if the three of them might form a club, perhaps the Cool Ducks?

It was a beautiful spring day, but Gina felt chilly. She wished she'd brought her sweater outside with her. She stopped and touched Priscilla's arm, pointing back at the classroom.

"What's wrong? Did you forget something?" Priscilla asked.

Gina nodded.

"Well, let's go back and get it," said Priscilla.

When they got back to the classroom, they saw Kylie standing at Ms. Armstrong's desk. She was reading the Young Authors' stories. Ms. Armstrong wasn't there. Gina froze, and Priscilla rushed over.

"Hey!" said Priscilla. "What do you think you're doing? You're not supposed to be reading those!"

Kylie looked up nervously. Then she saw who was speaking. "I just read yours, Priscilla. Two pages? We've been working on these for nearly a month!"

Priscilla strode across the room and towered over Kylie. Gina followed. "It's three pages, you liar!" Priscilla said. "Who asked you to read other people's stories?"

"Well, at least *I* wrote my *own*," Kylie said snidely, glancing sideways at Gina. "At least *I* didn't copy mine from a *book*."

"What's that supposed to mean?" Priscilla looked confused.

"Isn't it obvious? Gina can't speak a single word of English! How could she write a story like this?" Kylie had Gina's rough draft in her hand.

"Did you read that?" Priscilla asked.

"Yeah, and I read it last year, too, in the library. It's

word-for-word, the exact same story, about the Monkey King. Gina's dumb if she doesn't think Ms. Armstrong will notice."

Priscilla looked at Gina with uncertainty. Gina shook her head no, vigorously. The Princess poked her head out of Gina's pocket as if to protest.

"That's not true. Gina made up that whole story," Priscilla said. "I know."

"How could you know?" said Kylie. "Look at this." She showed Priscilla a page from the story. "'Monkey swirled and twirled and transformed himself into a snake,'" she read. "How could Gina Zhang write a sentence like that, when she can't even say 'Hello. My name is Gina'?"

Priscilla's face grew red and her voice grew loud. "Well, I helped her with some of the words, but the story is hers. Completely hers."

"Right. The reason Gina's story is so good is because *you* helped her. Yeah, and I'm a teenage singing sensation. That's a good one!" Kylie snorted. "Sheliya!" she shouted out across the room as some of the kids started coming in from recess. "You gotta hear Priscilla's latest joke."

"You shut up, Kylie Anderson." Priscilla's voice got louder. "If you know what's good for you, you'll just be quiet."

"Oh, this is rich," said Kylie. "We're supposed to

believe that Gina sat down and told you this long, involved story, and you helped her write it up in perfect English. Right!" Kylie was laughing so hard she almost fell over.

Gina could see a fuse burning inside Priscilla. It first lit up her eyes, then it pulsed through her veins until it filled every muscle of her arms and legs, which exploded out toward Kylie. Priscilla grabbed Kylie by the neck and knocked her to the floor. Kylie let out a garbled scream and tried to pry off Priscilla's fingers. But Priscilla was on top of her, all one hundred pounds of her, banging Kylie's wavy-haired blond head into the hard, gray carpet. Kylie's legs kicked and flailed.

"You just shut up, Kylie! It's not true! You're a liar!" Priscilla was shouting.

Gina rushed over and tried to pry Priscilla's fingers off Kylie's throat, which was starting to look as squeezed as her own felt. Kylie's eyes were bulging, and Gina was afraid she would stop breathing.

A lot of kids, especially boys, gathered around and started shouting, "Fight! Fight! Two girls fighting!"

"I hate you, Kylie! I *hate* you, I *hate* you, I *hate* you." Every time Priscilla said the word *hate,* she shoved Kylie against the floor.

Gina shrank back from the fight, covered her ears, and screamed.

Suddenly Ms. Armstrong appeared and grabbed Priscilla's wrists. "Priscilla. Let go immediately." Ms. Armstrong's voice was firm but calm. Everyone but Gina fell silent.

"AAAAAH . . ." Gina's scream echoed in the classroom, and all sets of eyes fixed on her face. It was the first time anyone had heard her voice. She stopped midscream and opened her eyes to see all of those American faces, dark- and light-skinned, brown eyes and blue, black hair and blond, all staring at her in curiosity and horror. She turned to run.

But Ms. Armstrong reached up with her free hand and grabbed Gina's wrist before she could get away.

Kylie found her voice quickly as soon as Priscilla's hands were removed from her throat. "She started it, Ms. Armstrong, you know that!" Kylie said. "Gina copied her story from a book, and Priscilla is lying about it."

The rough draft of Gina's story lay scattered on the floor, wrinkled and stepped on. Gina was horrified—especially when she noticed Pigsy in the midst of the mess. He had fallen out of her pocket. He would, of course, enjoy this kind of fight. She reached down to grab him, but Kylie got there first.

Gina struggled desperately to reach Pigsy, but Ms. Armstrong held her back. The enemy had captured the Princess's loyal friend.

"Priscilla!" the teacher commanded. "Explain!"

All eyes turned to Priscilla now. "Kylie's awful, Ms. Armstrong. She was saying awful things. She's so mean!" Priscilla was nearly crying. No, she *was* crying. Gina closed her eyes and wished she could turn into a snake and slither away.

"OK, Kylie, you start. Tell me what happened." Ms. Armstrong's voice was calmer.

"I was flipping through some of the Young Authors' stories and I noticed that Gina's story was really long. I read part of it, and it was written in perfect English. It sounds just like a book I read last year. I think she copied it."

Gina noticed that Kylie was squeezing Pigsy. Could he breathe? She tried to swipe Pigsy out of Kylie's hand, but Kylie stuffed him into her pocket.

Priscilla shouted, "That's so wrong! Gina made up that story, the whole thing. She told it to me, and I helped her write it down. But it's still her story, isn't it?" she appealed to Ms. Armstrong. "I wasn't wrong to help her write it in good English, was I?"

Ms. Armstrong frowned. "Gina?" she asked. "Did you copy the story from a book? Or is it your story?"

All eyes were on Gina. She wanted to drink some of that liquid that Alice drank in Wonderland to make her shrink down so small no one could see her. She wanted to click her ruby slippers like Dorothy in

The Wizard of Oz and fly home. All these images from months of watching American TV filled her head. She pulled away, but Ms. Armstrong still held her wrist.

"Gina? Speak to me. Did you write this story?"

The metal band tightened and her throat felt inflamed again. *Yes, of course, it's my story!* She wanted so badly to tell them. *Stop looking at me like I'm some sort of strange foreign creature! Stop judging me! Leave me alone!* She opened her mouth, but the words wouldn't come out. She couldn't even nod her head. It was too complicated.

Gina's eyes locked on the floor and saw her words there, her own story, scattered and torn. She slipped her wrist out of Ms. Armstrong's grip and kneeled to gather up the pages of her story. Then she crumpled the pages into balls. It was a mistake to show the story to anyone. That was obvious now. Every time she spoke out and revealed a part of herself, she got into trouble. Why should things be any different in America than in China?

"Stop!" Ms. Armstrong shouted. Then she sighed. Her voice sounded exhausted. "All three of you, go to Mr. Caccamo's office immediately and tell him what happened. Gina, leave those pages here."

"You're such a faker, Gina," Kylie mumbled under her breath as they walked down the hall. "You can probably talk just fine. But you can't get away with copying. It doesn't work that way in America."

"You don't know anything about Gina, Kylie Anderson," said Priscilla, a little louder. "You think she's like Michelle, but she's not. She would never stop being my friend."

Gina walked between them. They were taking the same route that she had taken the first day of school, when she had tried to escape. Maybe she could escape now? She walked faster, almost running.

But Kylie grabbed her arm. "No you don't, cheater," Kylie said.

Mr. Caccamo was surprised to see them, two red angry faces and a pale frightened one. He closed the door behind them.

"You're not here for our lunch bunch," he said, but no one laughed. They all looked at the squares on his carpet. "OK, have a seat and tell me about it."

The three girls sat at his table, facing him, like criminals before a judge. His bushy eyebrows jumped up and down as first Kylie, then Priscilla, told him what happened. Gina wondered if she would get into even deeper trouble this time. The key was to say nothing. Or was it?

"How do you know it's Gina's story?" he asked Priscilla. "Have you heard Gina speak in English?"

This was a problem. What would she tell him? Gina looked at Priscilla to see how she would answer.

"Yes," Priscilla said reluctantly.

"Where?"

"At—at her house. And mine." Would they believe her?

"Not at school?"

"No. Not at school."

"And she tells you stories?"

"Not exactly. She . . . Do I have to tell you this in front of Kylie?"

"Kylie?" asked Mr. Caccamo. "Have you finished your side of the story?"

"Yes, but I want to hear hers. It's only fair. She heard mine. She's just making hers up."

"I am not!" Priscilla's eyes flashed.

"Calm down," said Mr. Caccamo. "Tell me."

Priscilla looked imploringly at Gina. "Can I tell? Please?" Gina thought about Pigsy, squashed in Kylie's pocket, and she gave a tiny nod.

Sighing, Priscilla began to speak. She didn't give all the details, but she told how she had first over-heard Gina in her bedroom. She told about the Yarn People. She told the bare outline of the story, about Princess Jade-Blossom, the Crow, Monkey King, and Pigsy. She told about the three tests and how she had typed up the story. She left out Dorothy.

Once Gina heard her give away the secret about the Yarn People, she stopped listening and escaped back into her head. She would start a new story, she decided. This story was ruined anyway. She would throw away all the Yarn People who had gotten wet, and she would start a new story about . . . Dorothy. Yes, that's right. She'd make a new Dorothy, much more attractive than the old one, with a blue dress and a multicolored belt, and she would be the main character. She would be brave and good-hearted and stand up for her friends. She would be smart and talkative and funny, but never fight and never poke people with sticks.

"Does she ever bring these Yarn People to school?" Mr. Caccamo asked.

The question brought Gina back into the room. She turned and looked Kylie straight in the eye. She put out her hand, palm up, as if to say, "Give it back." But no words came out.

"Kylie?" Mr. Caccamo asked gently.

Reluctantly, Kylie put her hand in her pocket and pulled out Pigsy. He looked terrible, like he'd been through a flood and a war. Of course, he had. Gina grabbed him and held him tightly.

"I still don't believe her story," Kylie said. "Just ask the librarian. There's a story about a pig and a Monkey King in the library."

"You don't know what you're talking about!" shouted Priscilla.

"Shhh," said Mr. Caccamo. "Gina," he said softly, "we need you. I don't know who's telling the truth. If you copied parts of the story, I understand. It certainly wouldn't be the first time a student has done that. Don't worry about it. But it's time to tell your side of the story."

Gina wanted to melt. Part of her wanted to shout, *What's with you people? Do you think I'm not smart enough to make up a story?* Another part of her wanted to fly out of the room on the back of a crow.

"She can't talk in school, you know that!" protested Priscilla. "It's not right to force her to speak."

"Shhh, Priscilla. Give her a chance."

Gina shifted her feet and put Pigsy in her pocket. He shouldn't have to witness this humiliation.

"Gina, did you copy your story from a book?" Mr. Caccamo had the kindest way of accusing a student of plagiarism. His brown eyes locked on hers.

Gina paused, then shook her head no.

"Did you make up the story yourself?"

She nodded.

"Did you write it yourself?"

She hesitated, then looked at Priscilla.

"Did you get some help writing it?"

Gina pointed at Priscilla.

"Ha! That's a joke!" said Kylie. "There's no way Priscilla could help write a story that good."

"Kylie. Priscilla. Thank you so much for talking with me today," he said. "You two can go back to your classroom now."

Gina reached out and grabbed Priscilla's arm.

"I'm not going back without Gina," said Priscilla. "We're in this thing together, and she can't explain it herself."

The bushy eyebrows met in a frown. "Gina will be fine, Priscilla. Go back to class now."

"Sorry," Priscilla whispered to Gina. "I didn't mean to give away the secret." She looked very sad.

As soon as the two girls had left, Mr. Caccamo turned to Gina. "May I see your little creature again, please?"

Gina didn't want to expose Pigsy again, but she reached in her pocket and pulled him out. Mr. Caccamo saw a bit of pink yarn, too.

"Is there someone else in your pocket?" he asked.

Gina reluctantly pulled out the Princess and Monkey King, too. She looked at the face of the person now examining her bedraggled Yarn People. Mr. Caccamo had told her parents she had a problem, that she wasn't normal. He had recommended she join the Special Needs class and made her face Meanie, Miney, and Moe. He had convinced her father that she was sick and needed medication. And now this man was asking her to speak to defend herself. How could he give her a fair hearing?

But when Mr. Caccamo spoke again, he did not talk to Gina. Instead, he addressed the Princess.

"Are you, by any chance, the Princess Jade-Blossom, of the City of Eternal Peace?"

His words shot through Gina like a jolt of lightning. The Princess was the daughter of a king! She wouldn't stoop down to speak to a man who had treated Gina so badly. Gina grabbed the Princess and held her close to her chest, as if to protect her.

"I won't hurt her," said Mr. Caccamo.

Slowly, Gina placed Princess Jade-Blossom high on a pedestal, on top of Mr. Caccamo's printer. There she could watch the proceedings from above, out of harm's way. Then Gina took Pigsy in her hand. He faced Mr. Caccamo.

"Are you the famous Pigsy?" he asked. "Why won't the Princess answer me?"

Gina didn't want Mr. Caccamo to hear the Princess speak anything but absolutely perfect English, and Gina knew she couldn't do that yet. Maybe Pigsy could speak for her. No one expected him to be perfect.

"She is the main character in the story, right?" Mr. Caccamo continued.

"Me, too," squeaked Pigsy, insulted that anyone would think he wasn't important in the story. He was on almost every page.

"I wish I could meet the Princess and get her to talk to me," said Mr. Caccamo. "Is she scared?"

"No! Brave!" insisted Pigsy. "She kill monster. She cross river."

"Did those stories come from a book?"

This question worried Gina. "Monkey King and Pigsy, we in book," Pigsy admitted. Would this get her in trouble? "But not Princess. You look at book. Different story." Pigsy danced around to make sure Mr. Caccamo wouldn't look at Gina.

"We have a girl at our school who is like the Princess," Mr. Caccamo told Pigsy.

"No. No one here as good as Princess," Pigsy said.

"Yes, we do. Her name is Gina, and she is very good at thinking up stories. One of the best in our school."

"No, Gina dumb girl. Everybody say so."

"I disagree, Pigsy. Gina's very smart. She must be, if she thought up a story like this. And she's also brave and kind. She stands up for her friends when people are mean to them. I suggest you go back to class with her now and watch."

Mr. Caccamo gently picked up Pigsy, Monkey King, and the Princess and gave them back to Gina.

"All three of you, go back to class with Gina now."

Gina held the Yarn People a moment in the palms of her hands, looking at them and at Mr. Caccamo.

"Go ahead, Gina," he said softly. "You need to explain to Ms. Armstrong and your classmates so they will know who was telling the truth, Priscilla or Kylie. I can't help you with this. You need to do it by yourself."

On the way back to class, Gina thought about Priscilla and Kylie. Mr. Caccamo wanted her to speak up for herself and to defend her friend, but how? How could she do that with the metal band around her throat? Would it miraculously fall off, just because she wanted it to?

She stopped in the girls' room to test out her voice. If Pigsy could speak in school, maybe Gina could too. She tried to speak to Pigsy. *It's my story,* she tried to say. *Priscilla helped me write it down.*

Speak up! said Pigsy. *I can't hear you.*

Just then, a little girl walked into the girls' room and looked at Gina with curiosity. "Hi," the girl said.

Hi, Gina's lips tried to say, but the sound didn't come out. If she couldn't talk to a first-grade girl, how could Gina speak to Ms. Armstrong in front of the whole class?

She washed her hands for a long time, staring at her reflection in the mirror. This was the outside of

Gina. This was all that the teachers and kids saw of her. Only Priscilla had any idea who the real Gina Zhang was. If Gina didn't say something to Ms. Armstrong, Priscilla would look like a liar, and Kylie would win. Gina had to speak up. But her throat wasn't going to work any better today than it did that first day of school. It wasn't as if she had a choice. What could she do?

She lined up the Princess, Monkey King, and Pigsy under the mirror and waited for an answer.

"Tell them," said the Princess.

"Yes, stand up for your friend," said Pigsy.

"Use your imagination," said Monkey King. "There are many ways."

Gina suddenly had an idea. She turned off the water and wiped her hands on a towel. Could she do it? She would have to. It was the only way.

Back in the classroom, Gina slipped into her seat quietly. The other kids were doing a work sheet about ecosystems, answering questions about their terrariums. Priscilla looked at her with a big question mark on her face. Gina shrugged and got to work. One of her sow bugs was hardly moving. She wondered if it had enough air, in that Coke-bottle ecosystem.

Ms. Armstrong came over to Gina. She had flattened out the pages of her story and read them, and now she handed them back to Gina. She quietly asked what had happened in Mr. Caccamo's office.

Gina picked up a pencil and found a piece of blank notebook paper.

It is my story, Gina wrote on the paper, forming her letters slowly and carefully. **But end is not rite. I rite good one and show you tommorror. OK?**

A wave of relief washed over Ms. Armstrong's face, and she hugged Gina's shoulder. At last Gina had spoken, even if it was only on paper.

"I believe you, Gina," said Ms. Armstrong. "It's a very good story. You can finish it tonight."

My frend, wrote Gina. She pointed to Priscilla, whose name she could not spell. Ms. Armstrong nodded, listening. Gina continued writing: **She help rite story. We share. OK?**

Gina knew that every student was supposed to write an original story. Two students had never worked on a story together before. But surely, she thought, if there was ever a time for Ms. Armstrong to make an exception to the rule, this would be it. Gina needed Priscilla's words, and Priscilla needed Gina's imagination. Gina looked at her teacher with pleading eyes.

Ms. Armstrong hesitated. She thought a moment and then nodded. "OK," she said. "You can share."

Chapter eighteen

PRISCILLA WALKED home with Gina after school, talking nonstop. "What a disaster! I'm so sorry. I hate that Kylie. I never should have written down your story. Will you forgive me? I didn't mean to get you into trouble."

But Gina was caught up in her own thoughts about the new ending. It had to work, and Priscilla had to get it. She needed her more than ever.

They went straight to Gina's bedroom, and Gina took out the Princess, Pigsy, and Monkey King.

Priscilla shook her head. "I don't really feel like playing today."

High on Gina's dresser was a six-sided bamboo

box, about four inches high. She handed it to Priscilla, her heart churning with a mixture of mischief and excitement.

Wearily, Priscilla took it in her hand. "What's this?" she said. A tropical fishing village scene was sketched on the lid. She opened the lid, attached with a hinge. The box was lined with red felt. Inside was another six-sided bamboo box, smaller, with a similar scene on the lid, less faded. She slid the smaller box out and opened it. Inside was the smallest box, less than three inches high. She lifted it out and opened it.

Inside, against the red felt, lay six tiny beige Yarn Babies, wrapped in felt blankets of pink and blue. The girl babies had pink bows on their heads.

"I'm sorry. I can't figure out what's going on. Are these babies?"

Gina nodded. She took back the bamboo boxes and arranged them in a row on top of the dresser, closed, with the babies inside the smallest box. Then she reached up on the dresser and pulled down a big new Monster made of yarn, with Saran Wrap clothing. She made the Crystal Monster grab the bamboo box and drag it to the back of the dresser. Then she put the Princess in the glass jail.

"This is weird, Gina. I don't get it. What's the Saran Wrap guy got to do with the babies?"

Gina smiled and shook her head. She grabbed two handfuls of Yarn People and made them swarm outside the glass jail. She knocked on the glass with her fingernails, as if they were knocking. The story was welling up inside her, pushing against her throat.

"I'm sorry. I just can't imagine it. Can't you just tell me?"

"You see? No kids." The words burst out of Gina at last. "Big problem for the people. Monster take all the babies. Princess, she not see that!"

The Princess was standing up in her glass jail, alert and listening to the voices of the people of Far-Away, in the province of Over-the-Mountain.

The Princess was truly looking at the people of Far-Away for the first time, and their problem suddenly seemed obvious. No children. She hadn't seen even one since she arrived. Why hadn't she noticed before? She heard some of the mothers crying about what the Monster had done, and she knew she had to help them, somehow. This was the right way to prove herself noble. Not by speaking with elegant words and giving a long speech, but by listening to her people and helping them solve their problems.

But first the Princess had to get out of her jail.

"Monkey King! Monkey King! I finally get it!"

called the Princess. Gina picked up Monkey King and brought him over.

"Yes?" said Monkey King.

"I understand now. Monster took away babies. People crying, and I must help. If you let me out of jail, I will get babies back. I will be clever and brave and nobu. Please give me chance!"

Monkey King hesitated. "Last chance," he said. Then he leaped on top of the glass and used his magic to lift it high. The Princess ran out before he dropped it back down again.

"Sank you, great Sun Wukong," she said, bowing to him. "Now I show you."

The Princess jumped off the hill and raced across the floor to the bottom of a huge white cliff, Gina's dresser. "Dorossy, Pigsy, you help me!" she cried, and Priscilla made sure they raced after her. The Princess, Pigsy, and Dorothy stood at the bottom of the cliff, looking up.

"Too tall," said Pigsy.

"I agree. It's way too steep for us to climb," said Dorothy. "Should we make another one of those braid things?"

"Maybe Monster is on top. I go up with rake and we fight," said Pigsy.

"No, I go up, alone," said the Princess. "I no fight. But I win."

"He's a pretty scary-looking Monster. Are you sure you want to mess with him, Jade-Blossom?" said Dorothy.

"Dorossy," said the Princess. "You sink I can win?"

Dorothy was surprised at the question. "Well, of course I do."

"Why?"

"Because you always win, don't you? You're the main character."

"Maybe I lose."

"OK, Princess. You wanna pep talk? My mom gives me one almost every day. Here's yours. Listen up. Are you the true Princess?"

"Yes."

"Are you smart?"

The Princess nodded.

"No, she's gotta answer," said Priscilla, in her own voice. "Are you smart?" she repeated in Dorothy's voice.

"Yes." The Princess spoke softly.

"Are you, um, brave?"

"Yes."

"Are you—what's the third one? I forget." Priscilla used her own voice and looked Gina in the eye.

"Nobu," said Gina.

"Oh, yeah. Are you noble?"

"I try."

"OK then, Princess, you go up there and kick butt!" Gina gave her a funny look, and Dorothy tried to give the Princess a high five.

"Sanks, Dorossy," the Princess said. Then she began climbing. She couldn't reach the first drawer handle, so Pigsy and Dorothy helped. At first, the Princess's hand slipped off and she fell back to the ground. But on the second try, she held firm.

"Go, Princess!" shouted Dorothy.

It was just as far to the next drawer handle. How could the Princess do it on her own? But she did. She managed to climb to the next one and the next, till finally she reached the dizzying height of the top of the dresser.

Just as her hand reached the top, though, the Crystal Monster stepped on her hand. "Too late for you." He laughed wickedly. "No one likes you. See people?" He pointed at the townspeople, who were waiting across the valley in a big crowd. "They not believe in you. They know you will lose."

"I not afraid," said the Princess.

"So what? I bigger and meaner and louder, so I win. Ha! Ha!" He grabbed the Princess, captured her, opened the middle-sized bamboo box, and stuffed her inside.

"Oh, no! Now what?" said Priscilla, forgetting to use Dorothy's voice again.

From inside the box, the Princess asked a question: "Why you want babies?"

"Babies are mine now," the Crystal Monster said. "After they grow up, they do bad things for me."

"But they belong to the people of Far-Away," said the Princess, poking her pink head out of the box.

"Not now! They belong to me."

"You not good-hearted," said the Princess. "You cannot make them listen."

"You bad-heart one!" said the Crystal Monster.

"No. I will prove that you not good enough to raise them."

"How?"

The Princess had to think fast. She hadn't figured out exactly how to solve this.

"We make a bet," the Princess said. "We do test. You win, babies stay and I do everysing you say. You lose, babies go home."

The Crystal Monster frowned at her. Was it a trap? He couldn't tell. "No bet," he said. "You stay. Babies stay."

"Then my friends get all people of the land to attack you," said the Princess. "They put you in jail."

"You no scare me," said the Crystal Monster, shaking his Saran Wrap fiercely. "But anyway I will win. What is your bet?"

"Listen. Here is test," said the Princess, thinking

on her feet. "I stay in this box. You let out babies. Then you go in big box. We both talk to them. See if they come to me or to you."

"Bad test!" the Monster shouted. "They see me, they scared."

"OK, we close lids on boxes. They cannot see us, only hear voices. If they all come to me, you let them go home to moms and dads. If any one go to you, you are good fazzer to them. I will tell people that babies are happy here."

The Princess shut the lid of her box. The Crystal Monster hesitated. He lifted the lid of the small box and tilted it on its side, facing away from the other boxes. Then he ran to the biggest box, jumped inside, and closed the lid.

"That's a pretty stupid monster," commented Priscilla in a whisper.

"All monster stupid," whispered Gina.

"What if the babies fall off the cliff?" asked Priscilla.

"You watch."

The babies couldn't walk yet, so they crawled along on their stomachs. "Wah! Wah!" they cried.

"Come to me, sweet babies," said the Princess from inside her box.

"Baby come here! Come here!" said the Monster, from inside his.

The first baby began to crawl toward the boxes.

"Trust me. I will take you back to your mama," said the Princess.

"You stay here, get very rich," said the Monster. "Eat what you want. Tacos, hamburgers, chicken nuggets."

"And potato chips and candy bars," whispered Priscilla.

"I give you potato chip and candy bar," said the Monster.

"And cake and cookies and ice cream," Priscilla prompted.

"And cake and cookie and ice cream." The baby crawled toward the Monster's box.

Suddenly, the Princess began to sing—not in English but in Chinese, in Fujianese, a lullaby her mother used to sing to her. It was about going over a bridge to grandmother's house. The words were soft and soothing.

"I'll buy you tons of toys," the Monster continued, this time through Priscilla. "You can have a swing set and a playhouse and a pony. I'll get you Nintendo and computer games and in-line skates. You can have beautiful dolls and baseball gloves, and tickets to the Supersonics."

As Priscilla's monster voice went on and on, the Princess continued to sing her lullaby in Chinese.

Then she spoke softly to the babies in Fujian dialect, saying the soothing things mothers say when babies are upset.

The babies were confused. They crawled first toward the Princess, then toward the Monster. Finally, the smallest one went to the Princess and stayed. The middle-sized ones did, too. Only the biggest baby, a boy, was tempted by the Monster.

"I'll buy you guns!" said the Monster. "I will take you to see R-rated movies! I'll buy a pickup truck and teach you to drive it when you're twelve!"

The big baby wavered back and forth.

"Baby boy, come to me," said the Princess. "Stay in box with Monster, and you always scared and lonely. Come to me and I take you back to your family and friends, who love you."

Priscilla held her breath, watching the baby boy. Sure enough, he crawled over to the Princess's box, and she popped out and hugged all the babies.

"You cheat!" said the Monster. He popped out of his box and ran after the Princess and the babies. One of them, a girl, fell off the cliff. Dorothy was quick enough to catch her.

"It's OK, Princess!" Dorothy shouted. "We'll catch them!"

"No, you don't!" shouted the Crystal Monster. He lunged at the Princess, but she swept the rest of the babies off the cliff. They all landed in the arms of Pigsy and Dorothy, unhurt. They were made of yarn, after all.

Then the Princess grabbed the big Crystal Monster. He was strong, but she immediately pulled his arms behind his back so he couldn't get away. Then she stuffed him in the small box, which she put in the middle box, which she stuffed into the big box, so he would never get out again. "Say uncle!" she cried.

Her magic had returned to her. She jumped off the cliff and sailed and sailed through the air, flying more elegantly than any crow.

As she landed gently among the people of the Land of Far-Away, from the province of Over-the-Mountain, they swarmed across the square and surrounded the Princess and the babies.

"Yeay! You save babies!" they shouted.

"Hurrah for Princess Jade-Blossom! We'll make her our queen!"

"She'll be the Queen of Far-Away, in the province of Over-the-Mountain. We'll be loyal to her forever."

The people of Far-Away sang and danced and had a huge feast of Yakult and rice cakes, celebrating the safe return of their babies and the promise of their good new queen.

The Princess had never felt happier. She was still

a princess from the City of Eternal Peace, but now she would be a queen, too, in this Land of Far-Away.

By Young Authors' Day, on May fourteenth, the book was finished. Priscilla had typed up the new ending, and Gina had pasted the text and pictures into the blank book. It looked terrific. The girls changed the author line to read:

by Gina Zhang and Priscilla Ronquillo

Ms. Armstrong read their story to the whole class, from beginning to end. Ms. Linden came into the class to witness the event, and so did Mr. Caccamo and Ms. O'Connell.

The kids listened carefully. At first Gina was tense, expecting them to start giggling and taunting at any minute. But they didn't. Instead, they laughed and cheered at all the right moments.

At the very end, they clapped loud and long. Gina thought her heart would burst with happiness. The new ending worked perfectly.

Then Ms. Armstrong asked Gina to say a few words about the story. But Gina shook her head. She still hadn't spoken in class, not even one word whispered in Ms. O'Connell's ear.

"Won't you at least write something on the board,

just to tell us what you're thinking, Gina?" asked Ms. Armstrong.

Gina walked up to the board and picked up a marker. The kids were looking at her, but it was all right. Even if they thought she was dumb, she knew she could be smart and brave and nice.

The room was silent as Gina wrote, slowly and carefully:

Gess what!
I am normal kid.
Its hard for me to tok.
I still learn alot.
Please I learn my way, OK?

At first no one said anything. Then they all began jabbering at once.

"I always knew she was learning English," said Michelle.

"Me too," said Henry.

"Her story is the best," said Sheliya.

Gina smiled. From inside her pocket, so did the Princess.

Gina looked at her classmates. Those faces that had seemed so strange and frightening on the first day were now smiling at her expectantly. They looked familiar and friendly. And they all had names—Priscilla, Sheliya, Michelle, Kylie, Henry, Rickie, Caitlin, Ms. Armstrong, Mr. Caccamo.

Gina caught sight of Priscilla's funny gap-toothed grin and smiled back. Then, glancing quickly at the cover of her book to make sure she'd get the spelling just right, Gina turned and wrote:

Thank you, Priscilla.

Dori Jones Yang

Then

Now

Dori Jones Yang grew up in Youngstown, Ohio, the youngest of four kids. She wrote her first story when she was eight and won a citywide creative writing contest in sixth grade. She turned her writing talent into a career as an international magazine reporter, living in Asia for ten years, where she eventually met her husband. Their daughter, Emily, was born in Hong Kong. Today they live near Seattle, and Dori writes for *U.S. News and World Report.* As a former tutor of immigrant children, Dori hopes her book will help American kids see past the broken English of a quiet classmate from another country.